AF422880

Father's Friend

(a linked novel to the Father series)

by

Rhonda Hanson

Father's Friend

a linked novel to the
Father
Series

by

Rhonda Hanson

ISBN 979-8-218-37669-7

Copyright 2024

by

Grace Under Pressure Publishing
P.O. Box 337
Bell Buckle, TN 37020

From the Author...

This novel, linked to the Father series, though not an actual part of the series, was written at the request of family and friends who asked for just one more parting glimpse, before the door closes and locks.

Although it can either be read first, before the series, or last, when the reader has finished the series, I personally feel that reading it last gives the greatest impact.

Long before she met Joel Etheridge, Meredith Clark was a sixteen-year-old runaway who ended up in New Orleans and landed in a bad situation. On her nineteenth birthday, she once again fled, in the middle of the night, headed anywhere north. Father's Friend takes you on her journey to be called a friend of God.

To those readers who have been willing to extend grace, thank you for loving Meredith, even when she was hard to love.

Rhonda Hanson

"Tell me, are you sorry for the
miles that you have trod,
on your journey to be called
a friend of God?"

"Friend of God"
Rhonda Hanson

The beginning...

"*Today* was my birthday," she whispered to the stone-faced, solemn girl who stared back vacantly at her from the mirror. The two continued to gaze at each other with hollow eyes but, when a single tear began to find a path down Meredith Clark's cheeks, the girl in the mirror shed one, as well. It was the only contradiction in an otherwise impassive, cold demeanor, as they studied their ugly bruises that were even darker today, despite Meredith's attempts to hide them with concealer.

"Nineteen," she whispered again, turning away from her reflection, suddenly unable to look at herself. It didn't matter, anyway. She felt sick. She turned on the tap and leaned forward to splash cold water onto her face, then stayed hovered over the sink, too weary to straighten back up. She knew she was still bleeding. The cramping was supposed to subside in a bit. They had said it should. They said a lot of things, but no one had asked about her bruises.

The apartment was deathly quiet. There was no loud television blaring in the background, no sounds of shrill laughter and coarse jokes that usually filled the air, when her boyfriend's "buddies" were over. They were all gone now, and he had been only too glad to go with them. She knew, when he grabbed a small duffel bag and told her not to wait up, that he intended to be gone all night.

Meredith braved another look at the mirror but found no compassion in the accusing eyes of the girl who looked back. She really was alone, then.

She turned away and stared around at the bedroom without actually seeing it, as her mind returned to the same thoughts that had been brewing inside her all evening, thoughts that were suddenly becoming a plan. Meredith looked at the clock, surprised to realize that it was almost midnight. The evening had crawled by, tormenting her with the unrelenting reliving of the day's tragic events but now, instead of time slowly passing, it suddenly seemed to Meredith as if she were running out of it.

She mechanically began pulling her clothes out of the closet and dresser drawers and tossing them clumsily into whatever empty luggage she could find. She had to pause, every few minutes, to wait until a new wave of nausea passed, but she kept returning to the task at hand, until she had her things packed.

Meredith drew in a breath and tried to work out whether she had enough money to leave. She rummaged around a few places in the apartment where she had stumbled on cash before, and did manage to find just over two hundred dollars, but that was hardly enough to live on, even added to what she had in her purse.

She checked the time again and knew that the bar where she sang during the week was still open. They owed her some pay. She wasn't worried about running into her boyfriend there, since his friends had loudly announced their intention to go to a party in Belle Chasse, just south of New Orleans, and get, as one of them put it, "dog-faced drunk".

She reminded herself that she was also owed money from the cruise-line ads she had agreed to model for, but it was her boyfriend who actually handled all that and gave her the money, so she had no choice but to let it go. She wasn't about to call him and ask for it.

Meredith took one last look around the lavish apartment, certainly not with a sentimental desire to remain, but to assure herself that she could do without those things that hadn't fit into her bags. She felt a wave of disgust and repulsion wash over her and quickly grabbed her belongings and made her way out into the parking lot. She hurriedly shoved everything into her car, and locked herself in, not knowing what to do next.

After a long moment, she made herself drive a few minutes away to the bar she'd been singing at for the past few years, well before she was the legal age to even enter such a place. Even now, she was too young to buy a drink there, but that wasn't something she'd ever had a desire to do. She just sang her songs, drew a crowd, took her pay and left to go home to her dingy, sparse, upstairs dwelling that was unfortunately located over a smelly fish market.

It hadn't taken long for her boyfriend to spot the beautiful Meredith at the bar, and launch his campaign to win her for himself. He persisted for months, until he managed to convince her that he loved her, and coaxed her out of the depressing hovel she called home and into his very nice apartment. Meredith had no prior relationships with men to compare this one to, and naively just assumed that he was telling her the truth.

She didn't try to convince herself that she loved him, but she did allow herself to childishly imagine that they would share a comfortable life together, just the two of them. Because of this, she was unprepared for what life in this new home was really like.

It was a hive of confusing, constant activity that involved strangers coming in and out of the apartment at all hours. A couple of her boyfriend's "buddies" even had keys, so that Meredith was never sure when the door might open, and who would be coming in.

She recoiled at the bold way some of them openly appraised her, not even bothering to hide their leering from her boyfriend, who showed no reaction at all, other than to exhibit a smug confidence that she belonged to him.

"Not anymore," she muttered darkly. It was the only strong emotion that had surfaced all day, but she expressed it with a grim determination; the beginning of a simmer that would soon boil over into hatred and anger. She knew it was coming and braced herself for it.

She pulled her car into the bar's side lot and noted, with relief, that Cappy's truck was there. Cappy was actually Reginald Stoddard, an old, crusty bartender, who had spent his younger days as captain of several riverboats, but now whiled away his retirement pouring drinks and threatening potential troublemakers with just a look. The bar's owner was rarely on the premises and gave Cappy full rein. He was considered to be belligerent and abrasive, but he had a genuine fondness for Meredith and a protective attitude that always made her feel safe. In fact, if Cappy's truck had not been there, Meredith would probably have just continued on, having to make do with what little money she had on her.

She slipped quietly into the bar's back entrance and peered out from the small kitchen into the front. Cappy glanced over and spotted her with surprise.

"You ain't singin' tonight, are you, Merry?" he asked, pausing with his dishcloth in one hand.

She shook her head but continued to just stand there.

"Come over here," he directed. "I can already see it, but get over in the light and let me take a look."

Meredith reluctantly moved toward him and he peered closely at the ugly marks on her face, his own face taking on a fierce redness.

"I'll kill him," he said, simply. "He better not ever show his face in here again, or I'm goin' to jail!"

"Don't do that, Cappy," she pleaded softly. "I don't care about him, but I don't want anything to happen to you."

"You let me worry about that, girlie." He continued to inspect her with a chagrined expression in his eyes, then allowed his demeanor to soften with concern. "Did you tell him, then?"

She nodded miserably and failed to stop tears from escaping, only fanning the flames of her friend's anger.

"Listen, Merry, you don't need him. He ain't gonna step up, anyway. Only a real man would do that, and he ain't never gonna be a real man. I'll find a way to help you care for this little 'un, don't you worry."

She burst into hushed sobs and rested her head on Cappy's shoulder. "There's no little one, anymore," she said brokenly.

Shock and dismay swept across the old captain's face and he pulled back to look at her more closely. "What do you mean?" When she failed to answer him, he guided her chin to make her focus on him. "What did he make you do?"

"Don't make me say it," she whispered, her face a flood of pain.

Cappy wrapped his arms around her and comforted her in his own, awkward way, his mind racing, devising first one plan of revenge and then another.

"I'm leaving, Cappy," she told him, interrupting his thoughts with her quiet words. "But I was wondering if I could pick up my last pay, before I get on the road?"

He looked at her with a blend of misgiving and agreement. Regardless of his feelings about it, he knew it was for the best. "I'll count it out for you, girlie, but where are you headed? Are you sure you want to be taking off in the middle of the night, like this? Do you even have a plan?"

"North," she answered. "Just... north. Anywhere north."

He didn't blame her. He didn't like it, but he didn't blame her.

"I have a friend in Lafayette, where I can stay the rest of the night, once I get there," she volunteered. "She won't say anything, and it would only be for a few hours. Then I'll just start driving north."

"Back to Missouri?" Cappy knew this was her childhood home and the place she had run away from, when she was just sixteen. "You ain't goin' back into all that, are you?"

"I don't think so." She shook her head. "I'm not ready for that. But I just need to... I have to get away from him."

Cappy nodded and motioned for her to follow him to the safe. He retrieved what she was owed and tucked it carefully into her hand. "Don't flash this around," he advised, and she hurriedly shoved it into her pocket.

"You have my number," he reminded her. "You call me when you get to Lafayette, no matter what time it is."

She nodded, then impulsively wrapped her arms around him for a last hug. "Thank you, Cappy. I'll never forget you."

"See that you never do," he returned, a little brusquely, in order to cover his emotions. "You make sure to call me."

She gave him a tearful smile, then made her way back out to her car, slipping behind the wheel and locking the door, while she fished around for her phone, without finding it.

"I'll just take a chance," she breathed, and began her journey toward her friend's house, hoping she'd be given a bit of a rest while she worked out what was next.

Meredith had been driving for a couple of hours, since leaving her friend's apartment in Lafayette. She had arrived there just before three in the morning and Peg, her friend, had answered the door with a startled look in her eyes that quickly turned to concern. She welcomed Meredith inside, and pulled out the sofa bed in the living room for her. She was able to sleep, off and on, if only out of exhaustion and weakness, and it was almost ten o' clock before she finally got back on the road.

Peg had noticed her friend's bruises immediately and had a reaction not unlike Cappy's, but didn't ask questions. She didn't need to. She did, however, press Meredith for assurances that she was physically up to traveling, since it was clear that she was sick, but Meredith insisted that she was fine. She had dug through her bags after arriving and finally found her phone and had called Cappy to let him know she was safe. She made that same promise to Peg when she was ready to get back on the road, and left her with reluctance, but with a hug of gratitude.

Meredith's mind was a churning whirlpool of one thought after another, but nothing beneficial. No plan was presenting itself. She simply had nowhere to go. It was as this realization was bearing down on her that she heard a loud pop, and gripped the steering wheel in a panic to keep from losing control. She finally wrested her car over onto the shoulder of the highway and out of the way of other vehicles and closed her eyes tightly, to keep from crying. She knew without looking, that she had just blown a tire.

She sat still for a moment, trying to remember if her car had a jack and a spare. She hadn't had it that long, and had just assumed, when she bought it, that it came with all that. Now, she got out of the car with a sigh, and began the task of unloading her trunk, in order to determine if she had what she needed to change the tire.

She piled her things onto the side of Highway 165 and hoped that it wouldn't all tumble off into the ditch, then began trying to lift up the flooring in the trunk to see if there was a tire well underneath it.

To her dread and dismay, a truck pulled in just behind her. She felt a little less anxious though, when the driver turned out to be an older, white-haired man with a little girl, who also hopped out of the truck and followed him.

"My, my!" he exclaimed, with a friendly grin. "This ain't what you needed today, is it, Miss?"

Meredith found herself smiling, in spite of her misgivings. "Not really," she admitted.

"Do you have a spare?"

"I was just checking," she said, turning back to try to lift up the flooring. She finally got it raised and looked back at him with a hopeful expression. "There's a tire here!"

"Well, let me see what I can do to help," he offered, and simply reached for the tire before she could protest. He stopped and looked at her with a bit of disappointment.

"This tire's as flat as the one you just blew out," he stated regretfully.

Meredith let out a shaky breath and looked away, then hung her head, unsure of what to do.

"Tell you what," the man said briskly. "Carlyn and I are just out runnin' errands and there ain't nothing too important that we can't just tend to later. Oh," he added, "this is my girl, Carlyn."

He laid a hand on the little girl's shoulder with a beam of pride and she smiled up at Meredith shyly, with a quiet "hello".

"I'm Pastor Fred," he finished.

"A real pastor?" Meredith blurted out, before she could stop herself. She couldn't remember having ever met a pastor, before.

"I sure hope so!" he laughed. "Or else my church might end up runnin' me off!" He grinned at her, his eyes twinking in amusement. "Pastor Fred Blake," he said, holding his hand out to her.

Meredith shook it briefly. "I'm Meredith Clark," she replied. "Or Merry, I guess.   Some people just call me that."

"Like Merry Christmas?" Carlyn asked, her eyes lighting up in wonder.

Meredith surprised herself by laughing. "I guess so!"

"Why don't we just load your things into the back of my old truck and take both tires to get them patched up?" Pastor Fred offered. "I got a jackstand we can use to leave your car on. That'll make sure no one messes with it. I don't know anybody around here that's ambitious enough to try to steal a car on a jackstand." He laughed in such a humorous way that Meredith found herself laughing with him, if only a little.

"Well, if you're sure," she began and he waved his hand lightly through the air.

"It's just what the good Lord has laid out for my day," he declared, as if it were a simple fact, "and I'm glad to obey."

Meredith watched him in amazement, as he easily lifted up her bags and laid them carefully in the back of his pickup. She didn't know how to respond to such a strange statement. Was he still teasing her?

Carlyn hopped up into the cab and moved over to the middle to leave room for Meredith to climb up beside her. Pastor Fred silently noted the gingerly way she pulled herself up to get in, and saw the slight wince of pain that accompanied her effort, but wisely refrained from reaching out a hand to assist. He had also seen the bruises on her pretty face, where someone else had reached out his hand to her, but kept his grim observations to himself. He did ask for her keys to lock her car up and gave them back to her, before he started his truck and drove to a nearby garage.

Meredith looked around the tiny town, realizing that she had no idea where she was.

"Grayson," the kind pastor supplied, with a grin. "It's in Caldwell Parish. I'm just guessing you're not from here."

"No," she admitted. "Is it near Monroe?"

"About another forty minutes north," he replied. "Is that where you're trying to get to?"

"Well..." She stopped herself from confessing that she had no idea where she was trying to go. "I guess."

Pastor Fred glanced over at her with a sober expression but made no comment. Carlyn continued to steal little glances at the beautiful stranger sitting next to her then quickly looked away with a blush, when Meredith smiled over at her.

"Our little Carlyn's a bit shy, at first," her father informed Meredith. "But let her get used to you, and she'll talk your ears off!"

"Daddy," Carlyn grinned. "I don't do that."

He laughed and reached over to tug on one of his daughter's light brown braids. "That's just because your old dad never lets you get a word in edgewise!"

He pulled in at the garage and waved one of the employees over to his rolled down window.

"Howdy, Ward. How long you reckon it'd take to patch up a couple of flats?" he asked the young man, who couldn't stop himself from looking curiously at his passenger.

"Howdy, Pastor," he returned. "I guess not long, maybe about thirty minutes."

"Good deal!" Pastor Fred opened his door and stepped out. "They're right back here. I'm gonna pull in, soon as you got a bay open, since we got some suitcases back here."

"They should be alright, but you can lock 'em inside your cab, if Carlyn and your guest want to wait inside," Ward suggested.

Meredith had started to worry that she might need to get to a bathroom soon, and now nodded with relief. She and Carlyn got out and Carlyn settled down in the small lobby while Meredith made her way to the ladies' room.

Fred Blake watched her go with a thoughtful expression and a sigh. "I'm gonna need to use your phone, Ward," he said quietly.

Chapter Two

Meredith stood looking all around, scarcely daring to believe that she had just accepted the invitation from Pastor Fred to follow him and his daughter to their home. If she hadn't been feeling so weak and frail, she probably would have refused and tried to drive on to Monroe, but Pastor Fred told her that he'd called his wife, Miss Marcie, while her tires were being repaired and that she had insisted that they bring Meredith home to stay the night. He'd even offered to call home again and let Meredith speak with his wife, but she declined and finally thanked him quietly and agreed to follow them.

"Now, it's through the woods," Pastor Fred had warned her good-naturedly, after putting Meredith's luggage back into her trunk and returning her keys. "Would you like Carlyn to ride along with you, in case you need a little navigator?"

Carlyn's face brightened up so quickly that Meredith nodded, even though she wasn't sure she'd know how to talk to a child.

She'd asked Carlyn simple little questions about her hobbies and her life on their little farm, and Carlyn became more and more animated, so that Meredith found herself actually enjoying her company. Of all the things Carlyn shared with her, Meredith was most struck by the fact that the little nine-year-old girl was the piano player at their small church and that, like Meredith, she played by ear. When she let Carlyn know that they had this in common, the child was overjoyed.

If she hadn't had Carlyn in the car with her, Meredith might have been concerned when they turned off a little two-lane highway onto a dirt road, but she continued to follow Pastor Fred's truck down what eventually ended in an unpaved circle that surrounded a massive, towering oak and spread around near a tidy mailbox, and a fenced yard with a little gate. Nestled inside stood a charming, white, single-story farmhouse. Carlyn had pointed out the little green "Blake Lane" sign when they'd turned onto the dirt road, which explained why they had passed no other houses. The road was simply a mile-long country driveway.

"If somebody comes down this road, they're either comin' to see us, or they're lost," Pastor Fred declared, as he closed his truck door and came around to insist that Meredith let him carry whatever she needed from her trunk.

The screened door closed with a little bang, as Miss Marcie made her way down the brick pavers and out to the front gate. "Y'all get on in this house," she instructed, with a welcoming grin. "I got a fresh pot of coffee made and some sweet rolls just outta the oven!"

She made a beeline for Meredith and surprised her by folding her into a motherly hug. "Come on in, honey. I 'spect you're about wore out, what with everything you've been through today."

Meredith smiled at her feebly and Miss Marcie continued to fuss over her in her loving way. Her husband had confided to her, on the phone, about Meredith's bruises and the obvious pain she seemed to be in, so she deliberately appeared to take no notice of her condition, and only expressed sympathy over Meredith's flat tires.

"I got your room all ready," Miss Marcie announced, leading the way into the house and gesturing for her husband to take Meredith's luggage on down the hallway. "It's the next room after Carlyn's and then ours is at the end of the hall. I try to keep it tidy, even though we've hardly ever had anyone stay in it, what with Fred and Carlyn and me bein' about the only family there is."

"I sure appreciate your inviting me," Meredith said in a quiet voice. She was feeling a bit dizzy, from the lack of sleep, along with the harsh toll her body had just undergone, but drew in a deep breath to steady herself.

Miss Marcie looked at her over her glasses. "Sweetie, when's the last time you ate anything?"

Meredith hesitated. She couldn't remember.

"I thought so," the kind-hearted pastor's wife said, giving her a little pat. "You come on in and sit at the table and let's get you a little something to get your blood sugar up. As pretty as you are, you're looking a little peaked."

She pronounced it "peek-id" and her observation was made with so much kindness that Meredith could only smile and allow herself to be led into the kitchen.

Pastor Fred brought the coffee pot over and held it up suggestively. "Do you drink coffee, Merry?"

"Yes sir," she answered. Suddenly, coffee sounded wonderful. "Just black, please."

"That's the only way to drink it!" he approved. He poured out three cups and then shook the pot at his little girl. "How 'bout it, Carlyn Darlin'? It'll grow hair on your head!"

"I already have hair on my head, Daddy," she grinned. Her daddy was always teasing her and she loved it. She got up and retrieved the milk from the refrigerator.

"Get a little glass down for Merry, too," her mother instructed. "A little cold milk might keep that coffee from gettin' too rambunctious, when it gets to your stomach," she informed Meredith, with a little laugh.

"Mama, I thought you said you had some sweet rolls," Pastor Blake challenged, with a grin.

"I do, I just put 'em back in the oven to keep 'em warm."

Miss Marcie pulled the pan of rolls out of the oven and the kitchen immediately filled up with an aroma so wonderful that it triggered something in Meredith that she couldn't identify, but that was very healing to her heart. She sat smiling to herself, cradling her warm coffee cup in her hands.

"They're just a kind of hot cross bun, that my own mama used to make," Miss Marcie explained. "Nothing fancy, but sometimes simple is good."

"They smell amazing," Meredith assured her.

Miss Marcie served the rolls and then sat down with a look of satisfaction. "Now, honey, you may not feel much like eatin' but try to take in what you can. You need to build yourself up, for whatever the Lord has in store for you!"

She spoke as if Meredith knew who the Lord was, but her memories of hearing about God were very vague and had ended after her sweet mother died, when she was just a little older than Carlyn. Her mother knew God and loved Him, but they didn't go to church, since Mrs. Clark was too ill and never ventured from their home. When she passed away in her bed and was taken away by strangers, Meredith was immediately shipped off to live with relatives she'd never met and that was the end of any mention of God.

She knew to close her eyes now, though, as Pastor Fred offered up a brief prayer of thankfulness, then ate her roll, slowly but gladly. She did begin to feel a little less dizzy, but she was unable to hide her weariness.

"Now, sweetie..." Miss Marcie waved away Meredith's attempts to help put away the dishes when their snack was done. "You might not look like it, but I expect you're a grown woman and you don't need some ol' busybody like me in your business, so I'll just offer this as a suggestion, and then you do what you want."

Meredith waited, unsure of what was coming.

"If I was you, I'd go get me a nice hot shower and then put on some pajamas, and then climb into bed. Even if you're not sleepy, there's plenty of books to read in there, and that might just relax you enough to nod off. I'll bring you some supper, this evenin' and you can just have it right there in your room. Of course, you're sure welcome to join us out here, I'll leave that up to you. But I expect a little supper in bed and a good night's sleep might be just what you need."

Meredith flashed her a real smile and Miss Marcie knew that her idea was a good one.

"The bathroom's just across from your bedroom door, so you can just flit back and forth. There's plenty of towels, all layin' right where you can see 'em, and don't bother trying to clean up. Just hang your towel up on a hook and no one else will use it." She gave her a little pat of encouragement and Meredith smiled around the room and thanked them again, before slipping away to do as Miss Marcie had suggested.

She lingered in the comforting shower, trying to be mindful of how much hot water she was using, but unable to do much more than stand silently for a while, with her shoulders drooped and her head bowed. She was alone for the first time since leaving Lafayette, and there was no one to see her cry, so she let her tears mingle with the water and gave in to the relief that a good cry can sometimes bring.

After a bit, Meredith ended her shower and did as Miss Marcie said, climbing into bed, but not falling asleep, even though she so needed to. Instead, she looked up at the ceiling with troubled eyes and realized, with a stab of disappointment, that once she left this haven, there was nothing out there for her but a road she was suddenly reluctant to travel. She couldn't understand it. Last night, all she wanted to do was go. Anywhere. But here, in this loving, peaceful home, going away was something she dreaded and even feared.

But what could she do? She couldn't just ask to stay here. Meredith let out a shaky breath and wished she knew who she could talk to about all this, but there was no one.

A soft knock on the door was meant to test whether or not she was asleep, and Meredith invited whoever it was to open the door. Miss Marcie let herself in with a smile and a supper tray.

"Well, I was hopin' on one hand, that you'd be sound asleep but on the other hand, I was hopin' you'd be able to eat a good supper. Either way, it looks like it worked out."

Meredith smiled at her cheerful outlook and raised herself up into a sitting position, again wincing as she did. Miss Marcie noticed, but made no comment, other than to instruct her to "eat up".

"This is just a little potato soup, Merry, and corn muffins. It's pretty basic, but filling. I expect that's what you need. I'll check back in a bit and if you're asleep, I'll just pick up your tray, but you stay in bed, honey, and try to rest."

Miss Marcie moved toward the door, but turned around as Meredith thanked her for her kindness. She gave her a frank, direct look before saying what she had really come in to say.

"I don't know what you're dealing with, little lamb, and I don't expect it's any of my business, but I see more than I let on. You've been through somethin' pretty awful, that much is plain. All I want to say is that if there's anything Fred and I can do to help you with it, we're ready, on this end. Now, you're not a prisoner here, you can come and go as you like. But if you need a place to just rest up and figure out what happens next, you've got a place here, honey, for as long as you need. You can leave tomorrow or you can stay forever, or any span of time in between, but the fact is, you're welcome. If you do leave us though, don't sneak off. Let us send you off with a blessin'. But we're hopin' you'll stay awhile and heal up. That's all I want to say."

Her face creased with a tender smile and she left Meredith to ponder her words and to hopefully eat a good supper.

Meredith hadn't been able to respond and Miss Marcie had closed the door without anything more. She stared at the door for a long moment, then looked down at her tray. A lump formed in her throat and tears once again forced their way down her cheeks, but she wiped them away and allowed a small flicker of hope to begin to burn inside her heart.

After a while, the aroma of the soup became irresistable and Meredith slowly allowed herself to eat the supper that had been so lovingly prepared. She finished all of it, before setting the tray over to one side and laying back onto the pillows, looking up at a ceiling that became more gray, as evening gave way to night.

Meredith drifted into the first restful sleep she had known in a very long time, blissfully unaware of the persistent ringing of a phone she'd left in her car.

Chapter Three

Miss Marcie went about her housecleaning with a worried frown resting on her face. She had been in to clean the bathroom and had discovered the reason for their young houseguest's frail condition. When she picked up the small waste can and poured its contents into a large trash bag, what was hidden beneath the tissues tumbled out with it. Marcie Blake had just stood there, shaking her head, blinking back tears, and sending up silent prayers to God for help with Merry.

A woman's normal bleeding didn't look like this, and it wouldn't cause the alarming amount of paleness and exhaustion, or the expressions of physical pain, she'd seen flash across Meredith's face. Those dark bruises only served to reinforce what Miss Marcie suspected. She only had to look into the girl's beautiful, but sad, gray eyes to know that this was done to her, not by her, and that made her all the more indignant.

She carried the trash bag out to stuff it into a can near the back door, then turned to see Meredith hesitantly entering into the kitchen, looking around with uncertainty.

Miss Marcie gave her a welcoming smile. "I didn't want to wake you, sweet girl, since you were sleepin' so good, but now that you're up, come sit down and let's get some breakfast in you."

"Oh, I don't really need anything," Meredith protested softly. "Just maybe something to drink."

Miss Marcie dispensed with walking on eggshells, and came over to give her a little hug. "You need more than that, honey, and we both know it."

She gave her a discerning look and Meredith dropped her gaze to the floor, feeling a little exposed, but also strangely relieved.

"Listen," Miss Marcie said, in a firm, but loving way. "Fred and Carlyn are out in the fields, looking for a nest of bunnies Carlyn thought she saw, before we have someone come out to hay part of it. So it's just you and me."

She rested a hand on Meredith's arm and coaxed her over to take a seat at the kitchen table, then sat down next to her, to fix her with a maternal look. "Sometimes, things are just way more complicated that they first appear, and we have to ask for help from the Almighty to know how to see 'em. I been prayin' for you most of the night and this mornin' and Merry, I know you're in a bad way."

She reached over to lay her hand on Meredith's arm again, and the troubled young woman looked up at her with the day's first tears beginning to form.

"Honey, it's my belief that if you get in your car and take off again, you ain't got any idea where in the world to go to. Am I right?"

She looked down and nodded, but said nothing.

"Then what's the hurry?" Miss Marcie demanded quietly. "Why rush off to nowhere in particular, when you have a home and a family right here, for as long as you need us?"

"But you don't even know me," she whispered, looking down at her hands sorrowfully.

"God knows you, Merry, and that's good enough for us."

Meredith didn't know what to think about that, except to wonder how God could know her, when she didn't know God. She did try to talk to Him, when she was a little girl. She could remember being angry at Him when she'd begged Him not to let her mother die, and He did, anyway. After that, she had said some bitter things to Him, then never talked to Him again.

Miss Marcie seemed to read her thoughts. "He made you, honey, so He knows you. And we believe He brought you right to our door, to take care of you, especially right now."

"He never took care of me before," she answered, not in an angry way, but with a hopelessness that tugged at Marcie Blake's heart.

"He's had to love you from a distance, because there's been no relationship with Him, Merry, but He's done what He could, without overridin' that free will that we're all created with. When we don't invite Him to be involved in our decisions, we end up havin' to live with those decisions, and He's not gonna interfere with that. Still, He brings about people and circumstances in our lives to lead us to Him, and I believe that's what He's doin' here, with you."

Meredith looked at her with a flicker of hope in her otherwise dead eyes and Miss Marcie gave her a sweet smile.

"Time is somethin' you do have, darlin'. Why don't you spend a little of it here, while you work your way through things?"

"I couldn't pay you," Meredith admitted.

"And we wouldn't take it, if you could," Miss Marcie informed her firmly. "That's God usin' us, and we like to be used by God."

They both looked up, as Carlyn and her daddy stepped into the back door.

"Wait, Carlyn Darlin', and wipe your feet. Mama just cleaned these floors." Pastor Fred wiped his own feet and looked up with a friendly grin.

"Well, good mornin', Merry!"

"Good morning," she answered, with a little smile.

"Ya'll sit down," Pastor Fred's wife commanded, in her bossy, loving way. "I been keepin' a pan of biscuits warmin' and I already told Merry she needs some breakfast. I 'spect we all do."

"You don't have to tell us twice, does she, Carlyn?" her daddy said, and Carlyn shook her head and came over to sit by Meredith, with a shy little smile.

"Did you find any bunnies?" Meredith asked her gently.

"No," she admitted, with a sad, downcast expression.

"I seen signs that they'd been out there," Pastor Fred informed them. "But the mama must have heard we were comin' and hid 'em somewhere else." He winked over at his little girl.

"How are we gonna keep 'em from gettin' hurt, Daddy?" Carlyn asked, her bright, green eyes misting over with concern. "Can we just skip hayin' that field, this year?"

Pastor Fred brought over the coffee pot and waited until his wife had finished setting biscuits and gravy and eggs on the table, before he answered. "No, darlin', we can't do that, but there are ways to hay that field and still protect any of God's little creatures that might be livin' out there."

"How, Daddy?" she wondered, sitting up straight and waiting.

Pastor Fred grinned over at his wife. "Let's bow," he said, then offered up a simple prayer over their meal before continuing, while Miss Marcie handed him the plates to fill, and then send on around, until everyone had their breakfast in front of them.

"Well, darlin', we start in the very middle of that field," he explained. "We walk around in it first, to make sure there's nothin' livin' right there, and that's where we start to mow. We take our time and work in a circle, movin' out. That gives the little animals a chance to keep runnin' away, out to the edge of the field, without gettin' caught in the middle, and bein' trapped."

He cut his fork into his hot biscuit and paused with it halfway to his mouth. "We just take our time, like we should do with most everything. No need to rush, and that allows time to get to safety."

Carlyn glanced over at Meredith with a big grin that she couldn't help returning, as Pastor Fred's words seemed to line up with what Miss Marcie had been saying to her, especially when the pastor's wife sent her a smiling, silent reinforcement, over the top edge of her coffee cup.

"Fred, I been tryin' to talk Merry into puttin' up with us a spell longer," she said, in her usual out-in-the-open and frank manner. "Maybe you'd like a shot at it."

He laughed heartily and looked over at Meredith with genuine welcome. "You might as well settle in, Merry. If we need to, we can mow around your patch of high grass and that can just be your spot."

He gave her a little laugh of camaraderie and she smiled down at her breakfast, and suddenly realized that she was hungry.

Meredith stood looking around at what Miss Marcie had already christened "Merry's room" and breathed a grateful sigh of relief knowing that, at least for now, she didn't have to live out of suitcases. Those had all been stored in the attic for her by Pastor Fred, and her things were all either hanging now in her own closet, or had been folded neatly and placed into the beautiful, maple chifferobe.

She had laid a few personal items around the room; her journal, a music box, books of poetry and a mysterious, leather satchel, with no shoulder straps or a handle, but a belted buckle across the front, protecting what was inside.

She sat down and opened it and reached in to pull out an old Bible that would have fallen apart long ago, were it not for the shelter that the brown satchel provided. It belonged to her mother and had been given to her shortly before Mrs. Clark's health began to more rapidly deteriorate.

Lydia Clark's heart had failed her in more ways than one, first breaking with the loss of her husband and Meredith's father, Hollis, who drowned when his boat capsized in a swollen river, while Lydia was still carrying his child.

Her heart broke again, the day she called her little girl to her bedside and gave her the Bible, and told her that she would soon be going to live in Heaven, and that she wanted Meredith to be sure to always love God so that she and Meredith's daddy could see her again. Then, her tired, sick heart soon beat its last, and Lydia Clark was taken up into the arms of a God she had always loved and put her trust in, leaving little Meredith behind to be summarily dismissed into the care of an aunt and uncle who had no such regard for God and certainly not for His word, but who grudgingly allowed her to stay in their home until she was forced to flee.

Meredith opened the front cover of the old book and blinked back tears, as she read what her mother had written in a beautiful, but shaky script: *"To my beloved daughter, Meredith. I have loved singing with you, laughing with you and cherishing you with all my heart. Until we are together again, I am now, and will always be, your loving mother."*

She wiped away the tears that reading her mother's words always caused to flow and put the Bible back into the satchel, securing it with a firm, decisive hand.

Her mother had always loved God, but she had a sad life and died, anyway, Meredith reasoned. Surely loving God wasn't enough.

A soft knock on the door called her out of her dismal thoughts and she came over to open it, revealing a nervous but smiling little Carlyn.

"Did you want to see where I saw the bunnies?" she asked, twisting her fingers together in hopeful anticipation.

"In the field?" Meredith looked down at her bare feet. "Do I need boots or anything like that?"

Miss Marcie heard their exchange as she started from her own room with a laundry basket, to head into the bathroom. "No, Merry, it's dry out there, and nice and warm. It's a pretty, sunny day," she informed her with a look of satisfaction. "I might just ease outside myself, in a little bit. I still got some peas on the vine, and they need pickin' and shellin'. If you're cold-natured, I guess you might want a little thin jacket, but I doubt you'll need it, once the sun warms you up."

She moved on with her chores and Meredith paused, wondering if she should offer to help or go along with little Carlyn, who was still looking up at her with gentle pleading in her sweet, green eyes.

Carlyn's eyes won out, and Meredith grinned down at her and picked up her sneakers, before following her lead.

She stepped off the porch behind Carlyn and walked with her over to the side where a fence bordered their yard. She looked around for a gate, but Carlyn simply put her little foot into the sturdy wire and climbed over, since the yard fence had no barbed wire, as the field fence did.

Meredith shrugged and imitated Carlyn, although more slowly and carefully, noting, as she let herself over the fence and down into the field, that she was hurting less than she had been.

Carlyn had started on ahead, but stopped to look around for Meredith, who had halted in the inviting, sunlit field, to let her eyes travel across its quiet vastness of softly swaying vegetation and Queen Anne's Lace, and to breathe in the clean smell of the Bermuda grasses and the earthy scent of alfalfa. She closed her eyes for a moment, and thought about the smell. Scent had always been meaningful to Meredith, and seemed to always hint at something long ago and far away, that she could never quite realize, but always kept reaching for.

She opened her eyes as she began to hear something light and happy and musical.

"Do you hear that sound?" she asked Carlyn.

"It's over there," she replied, pointing first, and then moving off in that direction. "It's the branch."

"The branch?" Meredith wasn't sure what she meant, but followed after her until they came to a babbling, animated little brook that seemed to never stop dancing.

"That's what Daddy calls it," Carlyn informed her. "I asked him why once, because branches are up in trees, and he said 'cause it branched off a bigger creek farther up so, since the creek was there first, this one was just a branch. I like it," she added, with a happy, satisfied smile.

"I like it, too," Meredith admitted, squatting down and reaching her fingers into the cold, laughing water.

After a moment, she turned and looked up at Carlyn. "Is this the field your daddy is going to hay?" She hoped not. She liked it just as it was.

Carlyn seemed to know what prompted her question and shook her head with a delighted grin. "Oh no, we never mow the branch field. We mow over that way."

She pointed far toward the back of the property, where an old barn sat ready to receive the hay that would soon be gathered to store.

Meredith studied that field with a pleased little smile before looking up to find Carlyn wearing a similar expression.

"This is where I just sit, sometimes," she confided, in a loud whisper.

"Here? By the branch?" Meredith wondered.

"Yes, and also in the tall grass. Daddy said God is out here, so I keep a look out."

"What would you do if you saw Him?" Meredith was teasing, but Carlyn seemed to take her question seriously.

"Say howdy, I guess. And then maybe ask Him about stars and stuff like that."

Meredith pulled a stalk of Queen Anne's Lace and twirled it around absently, while she pondered Carlyn's words, with an amused little grin washing across her face.

As unlikely as it seemed, she found herself wondering if Carlyn was right and if God was out here.

Chapter Four

Pastor Fred came out onto the front porch with an old plastic colander in one hand and reached down into the brown paper grocery bag Miss Marcie had filled with purple hull peas. He pulled out a few bunches and settled down in his rocker next to his wife's favorite straight chair, and the both of them sat in silence for a few minutes, shelling peas and enjoying the nice day.

"Is Merry layin' down?" he asked. He pushed his thumb through the dark pods and let the peas run down the length and drop into the colander, before tossing each empty pod into another paper bag that was meant to be thrown away.

Marcie nodded out toward the field. "Yonder is her little head, stickin' up. You can just see her. It took me a while, but Carlyn said that's where she was, and I finally spotted her."

Pastor Fred stopped his rocker and raised himself up to look over his glasses for a moment, before a grin finally told Miss Marcie that he'd spotted her, as well.

"That grass is almost taller than she is. I'll have to tell her not to sit out there like that, during deer season."

Miss Marcie smiled and swatted his arm with an empty pea pod. "Ain't nobody hunts out on our land, and you know it, Fred Blake. Don't be scarin' that girl out of doin' somethin' she seems to enjoy."

"Reckon what it is about that old field that speaks to her," the pastor wondered out loud.

"Carlyn told her what you said about God bein' out there. Maybe she's hopin' He really is."

"Well, He might be." He smiled to himself and turned his attention back to shelling the peas for a moment, before his wife leaned toward him in a confidential way that meant for him to do the same.

"Fred..." She stopped and looked back toward the screen door to see if Carlyn was around.

"She's got my old guitar out on the back porch," her husband reassured her.

Miss Marcie nodded with relief. "I kinda pieced it all together right after Merry got here, but I waited, hopin' she'd tell me, herself, what she was dealin' with. But you know me. I finally just had to flat out tell her what I was thinkin' was the matter." She shook her head sadly, wishing she'd been wrong. "Merry had been livin' in New Orleans, singin' in a bar, before she came up here. Of course, I had no way of knowin' any of that. I found that out when we was talkin'. But I did suspect that she had been carryin' a baby, and she had been. But by the time she got here, it was gone."

Pastor Fred stopped rocking and stared down into the colander, listening intently, as his own suspicions were being confirmed.

"I thought maybe a miscarriage, at first. I guess I hoped that's what it was." Miss Marcie pulled a tissue out of her apron pocket and dabbed at her eyes and nose. "But them bruises on that sweet girl's face... that don't come with no miscarriage and I told her that."

She looked at her husband and her eyes were filled with grief. "She got beat up pretty bad and then she was made to go to one of them clinics. I tell you, Fred..." A flood of tears began running down the woman's face. "It's a wonder she even lived through it. It has to be God, that she even made it this far. That young 'un was so sick."

Fred Blake continued to stare furiously down at the peas, and blinked back his own tears. He didn't know what to say, so he said nothing, but what his wife had just told him broke his heart.

"We just have to be gentle with her," Marcie said softly, looking out toward Meredith, who sat silently in the sun with her head back and her eyes closed, listening to the wind in the tall grass, as if it were a song. "She has a lot of healin' up to do and not just her little body. But I made sure I told her that this is her safe place and that the Lord loves her, no matter what. I'm just prayin' she discovers that for herself."

Pastor Fred nodded, then reached over and patted his wife's cheek with a soft touch. "You're a good woman, Marcie Blake."

She sat silent for a moment, then looked away with a teasing smile. "Tell me something I don't know."

Meredith sat looking around the old church with wide, child-like eyes. She had never been inside a church before. Even when her mother passed, there had been no church funeral, just a graveside service with a few adults she didn't know and even that had only lasted a few moments.

She stared around now, taking it all in, from the old upright piano against one side wall of the platform stage, to the boxy old pulpit with a little service bell on one side and a bottle of some kind of clear oil on the other. It was all strange in a nice way, and filled with intriguing scents.

"It's nothin' fancy, but we like it." Pastor Fred smiled down at her. "Kinda like an old pair of shoes, I guess. It just fits us."

"I like it, too," Meredith said quietly, but sincerely.

"Well, I expect you've seen prettier ones," he observed.

"Actually, no," she admitted. "This is the first church I've ever been inside."

Pastor Blake raised his brows and laughed. "Well, then forget everything I just said. This is the finest little church you've ever seen!"

Meredith laughed with him. "It really is!"

He grinned and moved on down the aisle, looking for any left over tissues or gum wrappers or anything else that needed picking up.

"Can I help?" Meredith's meek question surprised him, but he didn't show it.

"Well, how ambitious are you with a feather duster?" he challenged and she grinned.

"I'm not ready to turn pro or anything," she joked. "But I'm better than nothing, I guess."

The pastor laughed and looked around for where that duster had gotten off to. He spied it and pointed.

"Yonder it is, on that altar, Merry. Now just take your time. We're just here to clean, we're not fixin' to have service today."

She looked toward where he'd pointed, with a confused expression. She didn't know where the altar was.

Pastor Fred smiled to himself. "See those two long wooden bench-like things up front, on either side?" He waited for her to nod. "Those are altars."

"But they just look like benches." Meredith thought she'd seen pictures of altars before and they'd always been large elaborate things.

"Actually, that's another name for this kind of altar," Pastor Fred informed her. "The mourner's bench."

Meredith repeated the term to herself softly. It had a poetic sound to it, although it also sounded very sad.

"Well..." Pastor Fred took a moment to sit down and looked thoughtfully at the altars, as if seeing them for the first time. He'd never been asked about them.

"Way back in the day, I expect maybe even as far back as Colonial times, they had these types of benches in the churches and that's where people would go and sit and sometimes kneel, which is the way folks do nowadays, and mourn for their sins and look for forgiveness. Back then, they'd just sit there and after the church service, the speaker and some of the church members would go over to the mourner's bench and comfort the ones mournin' over their sins and pray for 'em.

"Of course, even though folks still use 'em here, at our little church, they don't have to sit on 'em and wait for the service to be over, to get some prayer. As far as that goes, they can talk to Jesus about their sins just fine, from wherever they happen to be. These old altars are just here, though, for when a person has a broken and contrite spirit and just wants to get low."

He stood up and looked down at Meredith with a kind smile. "Come over to it, I want you to see something."

She followed him, a little unsure of herself, but trusting him not to lead her into anything unpleasant.

He knelt down at the altar and motioned for her to do the same, grinning at her reluctance. "We're not gonna pray or anything, I just want to see what this altar smells like to you."

Meredith was curious now, and lowered herself to kneel in front of it. She bent forward and put her face close to the old wood and thought about it, while she sniffed, then looked up at Pastor Fred with surprise.

"I smell salt." She drew her brows in confusion.

"That's right, salt. Tears," he added and she laid a hand on her heart and looked down at the altar with quiet respect.

Pastor Fred reached over and lifted the feather duster up and handed it to her with a smile.

She stood up and took it, then looked around for where to begin.

"Maybe start up front and work your way back to the vestibule," he suggested. "That way, you won't get run over by Miss Marcie's vacuum cleaner. I can hear her gainin' on us." He braced himself against the altar to get to his feet.

She grinned and stepped onto the platform, then looked over at the upright piano with a little pang. Her mother had an old upright piano. It was supposed to be in a storage facility but she doubted her aunt would have continued to pay for it. She let out a sigh of longing, then made herself start there, using the duster to slowly brush its surface, as she studied its lines and looked for its maker's mark.

Carlyn had come in with a trash bag and her face broke into a big smile. She let it drop to the floor and hurried up onto the platform to join Meredith.

"Will you play it?" she pleaded.

"Me?" Meredith said, with a teasing little grin. "You, first!"

"If I do, then will you? Really?"

It was the most excited Meredith had ever seen Carlyn become and she finally gave her a slight nod.

The child hurried to raise the fallboard and pull out the bench. "I can't reach the pedals yet," she apologized. "I can a little, if I sit on the front edge, but the bench always tries to tip over." She laughed at her own clumsiness, then settled down to play, stopping suddenly and drawing a blank. "I never can think what to play, when it's time."

"I have that problem, too," Meredith confessed.

"Why don't you play 'If I Knew Of A Land', Carlyn?" her dad suggested, coming around to join them.

She nodded and began to roll the chords and Pastor Fred couldn't resist singing to the old song. Meredith had never heard the words before, but the wistful lyrics about a land where no sorrows ever came and each verse ending with the plaintive "I would sell all I have and move today" touched her heart and she found herself wanting to learn it.

Miss Marcie had come in when she had stopped to move the vacuum plug to a closer outlet and heard the piano. She reached over and picked up a paperback hymnal and turned to the song, then handed it to Meredith, who looked down at it with delight in her eyes.

Pastor Fred continued to plow through the song, in his rugged, country voice and Miss Marcie provided a sturdy alto harmony. Meredith followed the words, as they sang, with tears in her eyes, and a faint little smile resting on her lips.

"I've never heard that," she admitted to them, when they were done. "It's beautiful. Do you ever sing it here?"

"We do, although not as often as I'd like," Pastor Fred replied.

"Carlyn, you really surprised me," Meredith said, causing the little piano player to flush with a mix of embarrassment and joy. "You play so well, it's hard to believe you're only nine!"

"God sure put a deposit in her!" her mother declared, with forgivable pride. "She's our little miracle."

"You promised to play," Carlyn reminded, hopping off the bench and begging silently with just a look.

"How do either of you ever say no to this child, when she looks at you like that?" Meredith demanded, with a little laugh.

Carlyn grinned self-consciously, but she still remained expectant that Meredith would keep her promise.

She pulled the bench back a little further and seated herself, then looked over at Carlyn with a grin. "You thought I was kidding about not knowing what to play either, but I wasn't."

"Do you remember any songs from when you were little?" Carlyn asked innocently, not realizing that her simple question pierced Meredith's heart with a slight sting.

She and her mother had always sung together. Meredith's mother, Lydia, had a beautiful voice, as lovely as her face was. She sang with heartfelt conviction and it was a sad day for little Meredith when her mother could no longer sing without coughing and struggling to get air.

Pastor Fred looked over at his wife and they both waited in silence, realizing that Meredith was working through a moment.

Finally, she laid hesitant fingers on the keys. "My mother passed when I was a little girl, but she used to sing this," she murmured softly, before moving her fingers over the keys, drawing the melody forth, her eyes closed, as she became caught up in a song she hadn't heard in many years.

No one had expected to hear the beautiful sound that came next, as Meredith forgot about the others and began to sing the words gently, much as her mother had once sung them.

Why should I feel discouraged?
Why should the shadows come?
Why should my heart be lonely
And long for Heaven and home,

When Jesus is my portion?
My constant Friend is He.
His eye is on the sparrow,
And I know He watches me.
His eye is on the sparrow,
And I know He watches me.

Pastor Fred and his family sat in stunned silence, as this lovely, young woman seemed to pour out her heart with this song. When she was done, there was a moment of absolute quiet, before Miss Marcie came around to pull Meredith into a tight embrace.

"You might not realize it, but you do know Him, sweetheart," she declared, blinking back tears. "You might not-a talked to Him since you was a little girl, but you know Him, alright. And He surely knows you!"

Chapter Five

$Carlyn$ was in school today, so Meredith was left to amuse herself without all the fascinating observations and unexpected opinions of her little braided philosopher. The big, yellow school bus had lumbered its way down the dirt road, heard long before it was seen, and collected her, but not before she impulsively ran back and surprised Meredith with a hug.

Meredith rocked herself slowly, with a second cup of coffee in her hands, and looked out across the fields with a feeling of contentment, perhaps for the first time in memory. She thought about that hug and her face was bathed in a tender smile. Carlyn was like a tonic to her, and she was always ready to stop whatever she was doing and allow herself to be led off by a little hand to see some new kitten or bloom or empty bird's nest.

She looked up as Pastor Fred and Miss Marcie brought their coffee out to the porch as well, and settled down into their customary chairs.

"Our little baby sure didn't want to go back to school," her daddy announced, as he raised his cup for a sip. "She was set on just stayin' here with you, but we finally convinced her to do her duty."

Meredith grinned and continued to drink her coffee and look around, noticing a few trees that seemed to want to give fall color a little earlier than the others.

"Of course, we'd rather just have her here with us all the time, and we thought about tryin' to home school her, since there ain't no Christian school close enough for her to go to, but Marcie didn't feel up to that task and besides, we pay close attention to what she's being told at school and we make sure that God's word is what takes root."

Miss Marcie smiled to herself, thinking about their precious little daughter. "I reckon it's not escaped your notice, Merry, that Fred and I are a might old to have a daughter Carlyn's age."

"Well, I don't really know how old either of you are," she began awkwardly, and Miss Marcie laughed with delight.

"I'm fifty-three and Fred's fifty-seven," she boasted. "We was married almost twenty-five years before Carlyn came along."

"Oh, we'd given up on havin' a young 'un," Pastor Fred commented, but not without glancing anxiously over at Meredith to determine if their conversation about children might be upsetting her. She seemed fine, so he continued.

"Miss Marcie had thought all hope of that was gone."

"I remember the day ol' Doc Causey told me I was in a family way," Miss Marcie said, with a twinkle in her eyes. "I told him to get back over to that medical school and do a little extra studyin' and he just laughed and told me to come back in about seven months and tell him that!" She sat her coffee cup down on a small tree stump she had long ago decided made a nice table, so it was allowed to stay on the porch.

"Carlyn is what they call a menopause baby," she informed Meredith. "But Fred called her 'All Aboard', because that train was definitely pullin' out of the station."

Meredith laughed, in spite of her efforts not to. Pastor Fred and Miss Marcie always seemed to be able to make her laugh.

They all sat there, each smiling for different reasons, while the morning sun grew warmer and the day, more inviting.

"How are you with a fishin' pole, Merry?" Pastor Fred asked, quite out of the blue.

She thought about it. "I haven't done any fishing since I was pretty little. My mother said my dad was a really good fisherman, but he died out on a river before I was born, so if I turn out to be any good at it, I guess that would come from him. She used to say that was why I seemed to like it, but I don't remember much about it."

"This'd be a good day to find out," Fred Blake observed, looking up at the sky and around at the field. "Marcie, what do you think? Catfish for supper?"

"I reckon I can spare some time for that," she agreed.

"I haven't seen many fish in the branch," Meredith said, looking out toward it with a furrowed brow. "Just some minnows and a couple of larger fish, but still not very big."

"I expect you're talking about little bream or maybe crappie," the pastor speculated. "Most of those stay up in the creek, but a few of them make their way down into the branch. They never get too big."

"We'll have to take the truck to get to any catfish," Miss Marcie explained.

"Well," her husband speculated, pausing to consider. "Of course, we'd probably do better out toward Woolen Lake or Beouf River, but for Merry's first time out, I reckon Castor Creek or Black Bayou is as good a place as any for her to get her feet wet."

"I'm not really gonna get my feet wet, am I?" she asked, only half joking.

Miss Marcie laughed. "Naw, honey, not unless you're like Fred, here, and you just wade on out there. I think

Castor Creek is less of an ordeal, for gettin' back and forth to the truck, if we're takin' a lunch, Fred."

"You're prob'ly right." He laughed and stood up. "Well, ordinarily, Carlyn would be disappointed to miss out on any kind of family activity, except for fishin'. She'll eat her weight in catfish, but she don't want to see 'em get hooked. That child is just too tenderhearted for all that. She won't mind at all, comin' in from school and seein' her mama rollin' catfish around in cornmeal, as long as she didn't have to see 'em die."

He swirled his last bit of coffee around in the bottom of his cup before tossing it out in the yard and turning to head back inside.

"I'll get you a pole rigged up, Merry, and let's all go see what we can rustle up."

Miss Marcie looked down at Merry's bare feet, with a grin. "You're gonna need something on those feet, darlin', and probably something else besides your tenny shoes. Do you have anything a little more sturdy that'll clean off, if you get a little mud on 'em?"

She thought about it. "I did have some hiking boots, but I don't remember seeing them, when I unpacked. Unless maybe they're in the car? I did grab a few last minute things and just threw them in a sack."

"You might wanna check and see, honey. Of course, if you can't find 'em, we can just put your tenny shoes in the wash, and I 'spect they'll come out all right, but if you have something a little more substantial and maybe a little more grippy, that'd be a good idea."

Meredith nodded and took her cup back in to the kitchen sink, before stopping by her room and getting her car keys. She didn't really know why she locked her car way out here, but it was a habit, so she knew she'd need the keys.

Miss Marcie was still sitting on the porch, enjoying the last bit of her coffee when Meredith came back and headed out to her car. She watched her looking around, then studied her closely when she saw her pick something up and look at it with a worried frown on her beautiful face. After a moment, she aggressively flung whatever it was down, and continued to search around until she did find her boots. She came back to the porch and noticed Miss Marcie's shrewd expression.

"My phone," she explained, in a sad voice. "I forget I even had it."

"People tryin' to find you?" Miss Marcie asked pointedly.

Meredith nodded.

"People you'd rather *not* find you?" she prodded gently.

She nodded again, and a little tear splashed down her cheek.

"Don't you worry about it, sweetie," Miss Marcie consoled, rising up out of her chair and drawing Meredith into a compassionate hug. "You don't have to put up with all that, and if that ol' phone is a nuisance, then I'd just fling that thing into the bottom of Castor Creek and be done with all of it."

Meredith rested her head on Miss Marcie's shoulder for a moment, before looking at her with a little grin. "I might just do that."

"Merry, this looks like a good, clear place for you to set up," Pastor Fred decided. "Now, it ain't turned cold yet, so I wouldn't be surprised if we see a snake or two, while we're out, but just keep your eyes peeled. This spot here is pretty open, so I don't expect one'll just mosey out and greet you, but I'd stay clear of these dead limbs and piles of brush."

She looked quickly around her feet and nodded before taking the pole Pastor Fred had already rigged up for her. "Do I use worms?" she asked.

He grinned. "You ain't afraid to bait your own hook, are you?"

"I don't think so," she said sincerely. "I think I can do it."

"Well, for catfish, let's try something a little less unpleasant than watchin' a worm squirmin' on the end of a hook, but not by a whole lot, I guess."

He reached into a plastic bag and pulled out a dark, stinky ball of something that Meredith smelled before she saw.

"Blood bait," he said, laughing at her expression. "If there's a catfish down there, he won't be able to resist it."

"Does it really have blood in it?" she asked, before reaching out her hand for it.

"I'm afraid so, but this is chicken blood, if that makes a difference."

Meredith didn't understand why the fact that the blood came from a chicken would make any difference at all, but she said nothing and let Pastor Fred drop the obnoxious mound into her hand.

"Now, look here, Merry," he said, reaching into his shirt pocket and bringing out a little scrap of what looked as if it had come from a pair of pantyhose. "Some of Marcie's ol' run hosiery," he grinned. "She saves 'em for me to cut into these little squares. It helps keep the blood bait on your hook. Otherwise, after a few casts, it all just comes apart, and you have to keep reloadin' this stinky mess."

He took the bait from her hand and showed her how to wrap it in the bit of nylon before working it onto the hook. "Now, I got you enough weight on that line for it to head on down pretty deep, so you just need to get your line swingin' out a little and then let it drop, where you think you want it. There's not a lot of limbs right here so hopefully, if you feel anything on there, it won't be a stick-a wood. Just watch for that bobber to go down under, outta sight."

Meredith followed his instructions and soon had her line in the water. Pastor Blake approved her cast. "That's just about perfect, hon."

He looked around to see if Miss Marcie had everything she needed, but she was a veteran and had already cast in and was keeping a watchful eye around her feet. Marcie Blake had never warmed to any form of Louisiana reptile, even though she'd been born and raised right in Caldwell Parish.

"Are there alligators out here?" Meredith asked, instinctively lifting her line every few minutes just to check it, even though she wasn't sure what she was checking for.

"Oh, there's 'gators pretty much everywhere," the pastor responded, laughing and gesturing around. "I reckon if we don't bother them, they won't bother us."

Meredith looked around to see if any of the cypress knees she saw sticking up were really alligator heads and almost missed the jerk on her line as the bobber disappeared.

Pastor Fred noticed and laid his own pole to one side. "Take your time," he cautioned. "But give him a good solid pull to set the hook before he gets too far off. Not a fast jerk, though. Just pull back, good an' hard, when you feel him takin' off with your line."

She felt the line growing tighter and gave a solid pull back toward herself.

"That's the way!" her coach encouraged. He reached over for a fishing net and moved closer to the bank. "Just keep walking back and bringin' him with you, Merry, and we'll see if we can't get him landed."

Meredith instinctively raised her pole higher, as she moved backward and it wasn't long before the angry catfish appeared in the muddy water on the bank and ended up being captured by Pastor Fred's net.

"I wish you'd look here, Marcie!" he crowed, with as much pride as if he'd caught the fish, himself. "Looks like Merry might have inherited some skills from her dad, after all!"

"Oh, he's a pretty one!" she agreed. "Now we're gonna hafta try to keep up with Merry, I reckon. She's already ahead of us."

Meredith grinned and watched carefully to see how Pastor Fred slipped some needle nose pliers out of his back pocket and held the large fish by the lip, while he used them to work the hook out of his mouth.

"You gotta watch this spine area, up near his head," Pastor Fred warned, tapping it with the pliers. "This boy's a good size, so it's not too bad, but the smaller they are, the more you gotta watch out. Those little rascals'll get you."

"What if you touch their whiskers?" she asked. She had heard somewhere that catfish whiskers would sting you.

"The only thing their whiskers are good for is to give 'em their name and maybe to make 'em look old. It's this fin area up near the head that matters, so I always just get 'em in a lip grip." He lifted the fish up by its lower lip to show her, then tossed it into an ice chest. "That's just my way."

He stood by while she baited her hook on her own this time, remembering how to wrap it in the nylon and thread it on. He nodded in satisfaction as she made another nice cast and then applied himself to his own rig, keeping an eye on whether or not his wife needed anything.

After they had landed quite a few fish, Miss Marcie led the way back out to the truck, where she produced a bar of soap and some wet towels from a trash bag, so that they could all wash their hands before eating the lunch she'd packed. Pastor Fred and Meredith pulled the aluminum folding lawn chairs from the back and set them up near the truck's tailgate and before long, they were seated comfortably, eating Miss Marcie's meatloaf sandwiches and already beginning to spin fishing stories.

"Well, Merry," the kind pastor said, in a way that she was beginning to learn came right before being teased, "reckon how good you are at frog giggin'?"

Miss Marcie shook with laughter. "You ain't takin' this poor child out for that, Fred, so you can just call Brother Lisenby or somebody else from the church to go with you, if you feel like you just gotta have some frog legs!"

Meredith smiled innocently at both of them, unsure of what frog gigging consisted of.

"I reckon you're right, Marcie." Fred Blake wiped his eyes and chuckled. "Castor Creek is alright for catfishin' in the day, but I guess haulin' Merry out to Beaucoup Swamp in the pitch-black dark, lookin' for big ol' bullfrogs might not be too fun for her."

"I'd rather not, please." She sounded alarmed and the sweet old couple laughed, causing her to laugh with them.

"You don't worry, sweetheart," Miss Marcie comforted. "As long as you got me in your corner, Pastor ain't got a chance in this world of takin' you froggin'. None of us females in his household are ever gonna be any use to him for that."

Her husband laughed as he pulled his pocket watch out and glanced at it, then raised himself to his feet and began folding his chair back up. "Speakin' of the females in our household, I reckon we need to ease on back before our little Carlyn's bus rolls in. She likes to know Daddy and Mama are right where she left 'em."

He swung the loaded ice chest up into the bed of the truck and looked around to see what else needed packing up and they were soon ready to drive back through the woods to the farm.

Meredith lifted her jacket up off the seat to sit down and felt something in the pocket, then stopped. "Oh!" She looked over at them apologetically. "I just... I forgot something. I'll be right back."

She hopped out of the truck and made her way back through the weeds to where they'd just been fishing, taking her jacket with her.

Pastor Fred looked surprised when he heard a loud splash, but Miss Marcie covered her mouth and tears of laughter crowded her eyes.

"Reckon she's okay?" he asked his wife, puzzled at her reaction to the noise.

"She is, now," Miss Marcie informed him, with a big grin.

Chapter Six

Meredith sat amid the tall grasses of the branch field, and let the sun and a southerly breeze rest on her face. Her long hair whipped gently around, as she closed her eyes and lifted her face and just listened to the music of the pasture.

She wondered if God might really come to the field, today. She'd never seriously believed what Carlyn had told her about that, but after what happened last night, she half-expected Him to show up and sit down next to her.

Meredith had always excused herself from going to the Blake's church and they hadn't urged her. Miss Marcie and Pastor Fred both realized that if she didn't come with them out of her own desire, then she would just be coming to try to please them, and they weren't going to coerce her.

Miss Marcie had actually confided to her husband that she personally felt that Meredith wouldn't be ready to come to church with them until her bruises were gone, and that she couldn't blame her, because more likely than not, some well-meaning, sympathetic, but misguided person could be counted on to ask her if she'd been in an accident.

Spending so much time in the sunny field had given Meredith a healthy tan and her bruises were now barely noticeable and could easily be covered with makeup, but she had still made no attempt to join them.

Last night, however, Miss Marcie was surprised when Meredith came into the kitchen and looked down at her jeans with concern washing across her face. "I don't own a dress," she confessed, glancing back up at her with apologies in her beautiful, gray eyes. "I mean, I have one, but I wouldn't wear it out. It doesn't have much of a top," she explained.

"What you're wearin' is fine, honey," Miss Marcie assured her, still not understanding why she was telling her this.

"But I mean..." She broke off and looked at what Miss Marcie had on, then back down at her jeans and the pastor's wife suddenly knew that Meredith was worried about what the church's dress code might be.

"Oh, honey, I'm just wearin' this dress 'cause I'm an old woman. The only time you see me in pants, is when I'm fishin' or workin' out in the garden, but that ain't because of some ol' religious thing. If I wore 'em to church, God would be just fine with it, although some of those poor people might wonder if ol' Sister Blake was touched in the head." She laughed and Meredith gave her an uncertain smile.

"It's just a comfort thing, with me, Merry. But we've had church work days and yard sales, and I usually wear pants, then. I 'spect Carlyn will wear what she had on at school today, and I know for sure there'll be women there with pants on, especially since it's a Wednesday night."

Meredith's face brightened and after supper, when the Blakes prepared to leave for church, instead of piling into the old pickup truck, Pastor Fred brought their big Buick out of the car shed, and she went with them.

The church service had all been very unexpected for Meredith, but not in an unpleasant way. Instead of the strange, stiff, liturgical type of service she had seen

Meredith knew she had heard this song before, but she had never paid attention to the words. Something about them seemed very personal, as if they were written to her.

She blinked back unexpected tears and tried to focus on the song itself, paying attention to the way little Carlyn was playing and lightly humming along.

When the song was over, Sister Lisenby called out another page number and Carlyn once again played an introduction. Meredith had never heard this song, and listened intently.

Once my soul was astray
From the Heavenly way.
I was wretched and as vile as could be.
But my Savior, in love,
Gave me peace from above.
When He reached down His Hand for me.

When my Savior reached down for me,
When He reached way down for me,
I was lost and undone,
Without God or His Son,
When He reached down His Hand for me.

Tears were coursing down Meredith's cheeks and she tried to keep them wiped dry before anyone else could notice, but it was no use. As the music continued to break in where no sermon had a chance, Meredith began to realize that she really was lost and undone, without God or His Son.

She was so caught up in the moment, that the song ended without her realizing it and Sister Lisenby called out the last song.

When Carlyn began playing the introduction to the very song that Meredith's mother sang to her every evening when she came in to say goodnight to her little girl, she began softly sobbing.

What a Friend we have in Jesus,
All our sins and griefs to bear.
What a privilege to carry
Everything to God in prayer.
Oh, what peace we often forfeit.
Oh, what needless pain we bear,
All because we do not carry
Everything to God in prayer.

When the song ended and Carlyn stepped down to reclaim her place next to Meredith, she wasn't there.

The child looked around and discovered her draped over the far end of the mourner's bench, crying out loud, as if her heart had broken in half, and Carlyn's mother was kneeling down beside her to rest her arm gently around her and help her cry.

Pastor Fred came to stand quietly nearby with a hand extended over them, praying softly under his breath, while his congregation did the same. After a long while, the good pastor signaled quietly to his flock that they were free to return to their homes, then came to rest on the mourner's bench next to where Carlyn had settled, while Miss Marcie tenderly ministered to a broken and poured out woman.

The tall, dry grass now began making a rhythmic, rustling sound and Meredith opened her eyes and looked around. All her senses were engaged and she suddenly felt on high alert, although she didn't know why.

She told herself it was just the wind, and maybe it was, but it sounded so much like someone walking through the grass that her heart began to pound in her chest. She thought it might be Carlyn, until she realized that she was still at school.

"Don't be afraid."

She jumped. She hadn't heard an actual voice, not out loud, but it was just as real as if she had. She almost stood up but instead, crouched even lower. It was then that she heard the waters of the branch calling out to her, coaxing her out of her uneasiness.

She took a deep breath and listened to its song and unconsciously began humming quietly to what had become an actual tune, with a distinct melody. As soon as she realized this, she stopped short and stared around again.

"Don't be afraid."

The words traveled down into her core and moved around in her spirit. She laid her hand on her heart.

"Is it You?" she whispered. "Are You here?"

"I Am."

She lifted both hands to her mouth and looked all around, tears rushing to her eyes.

"Don't be afraid."

"I can't help it," she confessed, shaking.

"Don't be afraid. I love you."

Meredith lowered her head and burst into the same salty tears she had poured out onto the mourner's bench the night before.

"Do you promise You love me?" she cried out, in a little gasp.

"Yes. You are my child."

She lifted her face but kept her eyes closed and took a deep breath. "If I'm Your child... does that mean You're my Father?"

"I Am."

Meredith involuntarily covered her stomach with her hands, and hung her head.

"Can You really forgive me?" she asked, in a painful, stricken voice.

"I have, child. All things have become new."

"I'm just so sorry!" She continued to cover her womb in shame, doubled over in grief.

"I know your heart," her Father soothed then repeated, "all things have become new."

The sun seemed to intensify its rays toward her and around her, so that Meredith felt as if she were being held. She let out a cleansing breath and although she kept her eyes tightly closed, she raised her tear-stained face up to the source of Love she could feel breathing down on her.

She was alone with her Father, except for the faraway, watchful eyes of the kind old couple who had brought this shattered, abused, young woman into their home and had been praying for this very moment.

"I guess you were right, Fred," his wife said, as he stepped up next to her on the side of the porch, to share her view. "It looks like God is out there, after all." She looked up at him with a smile lighting up her eyes. "Let's not ever mow that field."

Chapter Seven

Pastor Fred had dropped the females of his household off in downtown Columbia to shop and amuse themselves, while he headed on over to first pick up some feed for his chickens, and then go browse around a bait shop. He would inevitably run into people who would want to visit with him, so Miss Marcie knew they would have plenty of time to "mosey", as she put it.

The air had a briskness and a golden sheen to it, announcing that autumn had arrived. The Blakes had brought Meredith to Columbia the week before, for the annual Art and Folk Festival and she had been fascinated by all the artisans and food and live music. She kept a childlike look of wonder on her beautiful face all day, unaware that as she took it all in, she drew stares of admiration from anyone she encountered.

One of the artisans, who noticed the way Meredith seemed to be looking at everything with fresh eyes, stopped her as she wandered past her booth, and handed her a small wooden cross on a leather strap. She had simply reached out and caught Meredith's hand and tucked the handmade item into it and Meredith stared down at it, then looked up with a question in her beautiful eyes, before reaching to see if she had any money.

The artisan shook her head, with a light touch on Meredith's arm and a smile. "It's a gift, honey, just to let you know that Jesus loves you." Meredith impulsively gave the woman a hug and a sweet, tearful smile.

She wore the cross around her neck today, as she and Carlyn and Miss Marcie strolled the sidewalks and looked around at the various shops, stopping every few minutes so that Miss Marcie could exchange greetings with someone she knew.

When one of Miss Marcie's greetings began to develop into a full-blown conversation, Carlyn tugged at her sleeve, knowing she shouldn't interrupt, but risking it.

"Mama, can Merry and I go up on the levee?"

Her mother paused and glanced toward where she was pointing. "Well, honey, can you be careful and look out for cars? Every once in a while, one does drive up there, remember."

She nodded and flashed a happy smile before taking Meredith's hand and tugging her in the direction of the levee.

"Merry, keep an eye on her, darlin', and y'all try not to be but a few minutes."

Meredith reassured her, then allowed her little shadow to tow her toward the end of the main street and up the hill. When they reached the top, Meredith was surprised to notice that the street turned and continued across the top of the levee, but she was even more surprised at the wide, churning river that stretched out before her. This explained the bridge she had seen up ahead on Highway 165. They hadn't driven over it, so she hadn't yet seen the river.

"Is this Beouf River?" she asked Carlyn, remembering Pastor Fred mentioning it and pronouncing it "Bef", the way she'd heard it.

"No, this is the Ouachita," she replied, pronouncing it "wash-i-taw" and looking up at Meredith with a challenging grin. "Spell it!"

Meredith wrinkled her brow. "Wash, like washing dishes?"

Carlyn giggled and proceeded to spell the odd word, creating even more confusion on Meredith's face. "It's the name of an Indian tribe. They told us about it at school." She reached over and held onto Meredith's fingers with a look of empathy. "I spelled it wrong at school, that's how I know, now."

Meredith stared at the river for a long moment. "Does it go to the Mississippi River?"

Carlyn screwed up her mouth and tried to remember what she had learned at school. "It changes names before it does," she began, "into colors."

"Colors?" Meredith asked, smiling down at the great effort Carlyn was making to try to accommodate her. She finally looked up at the woman she had early on decided was her new big sister, with a pleased grin.

"Black River and Red River. And then Mississippi!"

Meredith was impressed. She let her eyes travel back out to the moving waters and watched someone off in the distance moving along close to its banks in a fishing boat. She wondered, for the first time, which river it was her dad had died in. No one had ever told her. She didn't think it would have been this one though, but it could have been the Mississippi. She felt a pang of sadness at not knowing.

Carlyn gave her hand a gentle tug. "Mama prob'ly is about ready for us to go back down," she advised and Meredith held on to her hand while they carefully made their way back down to Main Street.

Miss Marcie had finished her visiting and now waited for both girls to come back, before heading into a boutique she thought Meredith might be interested in. She smiled as they obediently returned fairly quickly, and gestured toward the shop.

"Merry, did you want to maybe take a look at any of the clothes in this little shop? Anything you have with you is fine, as far as wearin' to church, but I remember you tellin' me a while back that you only had the one dress. Did you want to look at any?"

Meredith's eyes lit up. She would have been ashamed for anyone here to see her in that dress Miss Marcie was talking about. When she had said it didn't have much of a top, she was understating things. It was something she'd worn to sing in at the bar, and she hadn't even realized that it had landed in her suitcases, until she unpacked. In fact, she had quietly hidden it in the trash.

"If you're sure we have time," she answered, and Miss Marcie laughed.

"What woman doesn't have time to go shoppin', honey? If we run out of time, we'll just make us some more time." She put an arm around Carlyn and gave her a little squeeze and a teasing wink. "I seem to remember this shop carryin' your size too, little lamb."

Carlyn's eyes began to shine like Meredith's and Miss Marcie opened the shop door and herded them on in.

Claire Michaels, the shop owner, came over to greet them with a warm welcome. "Miss Marcie! It's always good to see you stop by!" Her smiling eyes traveled over to Meredith and she glanced back at Marcie Blake with a question in them.

"This is Meredith Clark," Miss Marcie supplied, not bothering to offer anything more than that, other than adding, "She's stayin' with us, for a spell."

Claire Michaels took in the young woman's striking beauty and her own sense of fashion was stirred, as she realized that Meredith Clark would make anything in her shop look wonderful.

"It's so nice to meet you, Meredith," she said, reaching out to give her hand a little shake. "I hope you like my little shop. It's small, but hopefully, what it lacks in size, it makes up for in selection."

Meredith looked around and smiled. "It's very nice."

Claire beamed at her. "Just take your time, dear, and if you see anything you'd like to try on, the fitting rooms stay unlocked and each one has a 'vacant' or 'occupied' slide on the handle, to let you know. You can just come and go as you please and if you don't want to keep something, just hang it on the rack outside the door. But, of course, call on me, if you need any help."

Meredith thanked her quietly and began to move around the displays, as Claire then bent down to greet little Carlyn.

"I always love helping *you* find something pretty, sweet girl!"

That worked out nicely for Carlyn, who always loved finding something pretty, and Claire and her mother followed her around to see what would appeal to her. They had applied themselves so completely to dressing Carlyn, that they hadn't seen Meredith lift a couple of items from the racks and slip into the fitting rooms.

When she did emerge, she stood before the three-way mirror display and critically studied her reflection, unaware that the women's voices had become quiet.

"Turn around, darlin', and let us see," Miss Marcie suggested quietly and when Meredith obeyed, she and Claire Michaels drew in their breaths.

Meredith had chosen a tea-length flowing skirt with embroidered wildflowers scattered onto a sheer mesh backing, with a satin lining beneath that closely matched the color of the tall grasses she spent so much of her time resting in, when she visited with her Father. She'd added a simple, sleeveless, neutral shell top and a brown corduroy cropped jacket. The little wooden cross on its leather strap seemed to be the finishing touch. Meredith's long hair tumbled loosely down to her waist and she looked as if she'd just stepped off a fashion runway.

"Oh, Merry, you look beautiful!" Carlyn cried out, and ran up to get a closer look at her. "You look like a princess!"

Merry leaned down and planted a little kiss on her cheek. "Thank you, my little Carlyn," she whispered.

She had studied the price tags carefully before even allowing herself to try the garments. She felt she should hang on to as much of the cash she'd left New Orleans with as she could, knowing that, sooner or later, she'd have to start a more permanent life on her own, but the clothes were reasonably priced.

She looked at Miss Marcie, with a wordless request for counsel.

"Merry, this outfit was made for you, if anything ever was," she insisted. "If you don't buy it for yourself, then I'm gonna buy it for you!"

"Oh, no!" Meredith looked alarmed. "No, don't do that. I'll do it."

Claire Michaels spoke up quickly. "Meredith, if you would model that outfit for our web site and media page, I'll gladly give it to you!"

Meredith suddenly went pale and looked at Miss Marcie with panic in her eyes.

"Let's just buy it for now, and maybe she can get back to you later about modeling, Claire," Meredith's stand-in mother suggested.

Claire couldn't hide her disappointment but after Meredith and Carlyn put their own clothes back on, she graciously rang up both girl's purchases and gave them all a sweet smile as they made their way out of the store.

"It was so good to meet you, Meredith," she said, taking her hand and giving it a light squeeze. "And thank you so much for coming to my little shop. I loved seeing you in my fashions."

Meredith stopped and turned back in surprise. "Your fashions? Are you the designer?"

Claire blushed but nodded. "Guilty. I'm sort of like a starving artist, in that regard. I guess that makes me a little pushy, when someone as rare as you comes into my shop. You're a designer's dream. But I understand if you'd rather not and don't let that stop you from visiting again and letting me know if you need anything else, while you're here. And Meredith, I'm sorry if I made you uncomfortable by asking you about modeling."

Meredith seemed to be in thought before she looked up at the kind woman with a faint smile. "I'll pray about it."

Miss Marcie led her little flock across the street to the courthouse, and settled down on the large bench just outside to wait for her husband where she had told him he could find them. She turned to study Meredith with a knowing look.

"Claire Michaels is as sweet and decent a woman as any in this town," she said to her. "I heard her say she didn't mean to make you uncomfortable, Merry, and she was bein' sincere. If she'd-a had any idea she would have upset you, she wouldn't-a asked you about the modelin'. She meant that."

Meredith looked down at the pavement and nodded. "I could tell that she's very nice," she offered quietly. "It's not that."

"Well..." Miss Marcie glanced over at Carlyn who was grinning at the antics of a squirrel who had come just close enough to see if she had any snacks with her. "I 'spect this is connected with your life back in New Orleans and you're not obligated to have to tell me about it. But if you decide it might help to talk about it, maybe God'll drop some wisdom in me, for you. He's parted the Red Sea and knocked down the walls of Jericho, I reckon He can make something sensible come out of my old mouth, if He's a mind to."

Meredith laughed and reached over to hug her. "I reckon He can."

They stood as Pastor Fred pulled his truck next to the curb and gave them a grin and a wave. Carlyn fairly ran toward her daddy and hopped in to talk his ears off.

"If it was just her web site," Meredith began, and stopped when tears rushed to her eyes. "But she said media page, so I'm guessing she means something with a lot more views."

"And you don't want the wrong person viewin' it," Miss Marcie finished, perceptively.

Meredith nodded and hung her head.

"Well, honey," the sweet woman said, with a kind smile, "then they won't. Claire wouldn't want that for you, either. I should have realized right away why you'd hesitate the way you did and it makes all the sense in the world, now. Besides," she added. "I have my own suspicions about how God plans to use you, and I don't think it's gonna be modelin' clothes. I'm just puttin' that out there, for what it's worth."

"It's worth a lot." Meredith smiled through her tears. "I love you, Miss Marcie."

"Oh, go on with you," she grinned. "I love you back, so there. Come on, darlin', Fred's wearin' that fidgety grin. He thinks I forgot about feedin' him."

Chapter Eight

Fred Blake stomped his boots at the back door before coming in with his arms full. "Brother and Sister Babcock are gonna go ahead and pass out the food bank collection in the mornin', Marcie. I was headed to Columbia for our turkey, but they pulled up and handed me this one."

"Well, I thought I heard someone out there, but I figured it was prob'ly you leavin'," she commented, before looking up. "I hate I missed gettin' to see 'em."

He laid the Babcock's gift of a massive gobbler down on the kitchen counter with a grin of satisfaction that he only indulged in after his wife peered at it, first through the bottoms of her glasses, and then over the tops, and produced her own satisfied grin.

"That sure was good of 'em. I'll hafta give Bertie a call. He's a fine specimen," she pronounced, as Carlyn hopped up from the table and came over to look at their Thanksgiving meal's main entree.

"I'll get him in the oven, long about daylight tomorrow, and he'll be all ready to go."

Carlyn was clearly impressed. "How much does he weigh?" she breathed in wonder.

"Not as much as he did." Her dad laughed at his own joke and his wife shook her head and shooed them both out of her way.

"Where's Merry gotten off to?" Pastor Fred asked, going over to pull out a chair at the table and settle down a moment before heading out to split some firewood.

Miss Marcie smiled down at her kitchen tasks. "Well, now, where do you think she is, Fred?"

He looked surprised. "It's a mite cold to be sittin' out in that field."

"I stopped her and made her bundle up, when I saw her slippin' out," his wife returned. "And I made her take that ol' cow rug off the back porch, to put between her seat and that cold ground."

The pastor smiled complacently and pulled his glasses off to wipe them with the end of the tablecloth. "What's Carlyn Darlin' workin' on, so hard? Are you drawin' your daddy a Thanksgivin' picture, sugar?"

"I'm writing." She smiled up shyly and offered no further insight.

"If that's your letter to Santa, I can save you a stamp, since we all know the fastest way to get it to him," her dad laughed, and Carlyn looked up over the top of her notebook with a big grin.

"Oh, Daddy," was all she had to say, but that was enough to cause the old man to chuckle and push his way up from his comfortable chair.

"You might outta hold off on writin' a letter to Santa, anyway, darlin', since you didn't split your daddy no firewood."

She didn't say "oh, Daddy" again, but it was clearly in the look she gave him and it sent him out the back door in peals of laughter.

Carlyn returned to what she was doing, which was trying to write a song. When she found out that Meredith wrote songs and had even let her read a few of them, she began to long to be able write one, herself, and was trying her best to come up with something she could surprise her mentor and big sister with, by Christmas. She wanted it to be a gift to her.

Unfortunately, the arrival of a Thanksgiving turkey and a joking daddy had been enough of a distraction so that she was having difficulty feeling as inspired as she had been, when she'd first sat down at the table.

"Mama, is it okay if I go to my room?" she asked and Miss Marcie turned around in surprise.

"Are you feelin' okay, baby girl?"

"Yes, ma'am. Can I take Daddy's guitar in there?"

Her mother smiled at her. "Sure you can, Carly. Your daddy'll be back in here in a little bit with some firewood, and he ain't gonna let you just sit there, bein' quiet, when he can start some kinda nonsense with you, so you go on ahead, honey. I'll give him somethin' to do, so he won't interrupt."

Carlyn came over and gave her mother a hug before going to get her father's guitar out of the hall closet and take it into her room. Miss Marcie watched her go with another grin of satisfaction that was very similar to the one she'd just given the turkey.

Meredith smiled to herself as she remembered how Pastor Blake had warned her that Carlyn might talk her ears off and she wondered if Father would say the same thing about *her*.

The more she visited with Him, the more relaxed and open she became, until she sometimes worried that He was just waiting for a chance to "get a word in edgewise", as Pastor Fred put it.

Today, she thought she should just sit and wait and see if Father wanted to be the one to talk. She had already identified the loud chopping sound as being Pastor Fred in the yard, working on getting some firewood together. She peered across the field and could just see his green cap through the grass, but little else.

She'd been out in the field long enough to identify several of the birds who had been winging their way around her or perching on the nearby fence to look at her inquisitively, turning their heads first one way then another, before breaking into song, and taking flight again.

A Carolina wren had been entertaining her for most of the morning, but a beautiful red cardinal now came close and practiced his repertoire of songs for her enjoyment. Normally, he chose to encourage her with "cheer, cheer, cheer," but today he complimented her with "pretty, pretty, pretty," and she laughed.

"You're the one who's pretty," she insisted, then drew in a deep breath and continued to just sit and wait on Father to maybe say something, although there were plenty of things she wanted to say to Him, if He wanted to hear them, and He always seemed to want to.

The tinkling sound of the branch came to the forefront and seemed to entreat Meredith to hear its new song. She closed her eyes to listen and opened them again in wonder, as she once again realized that there was a cadence and a scale in its song.

"Are you singing to me, Father?" she whispered, after a bit.

"I Am," He replied, smiling down on her uplifted face.

"It's beautiful," she breathed.

"Yes."

She sat and listened intently, and wasn't at all surprised with the cardinal began to sing along with the waters of the branch and the grasses around her rustled with their own tempo.

After a while, the customary tears broke through and Meredith impulsively gushed out, "I'm sorry I took so long to know You, Father."

The music continued and He rested His gaze on his daughter. "I knew you. And I know you, now." After a moment, He continued. "You want to tell Me something."

"I guess You already know everything I'd want to tell You," she said, looking down at her hands and sighing.

"Do you not want to talk to Me, then?" He asked.

"No, I do, but... You already know, anyway."

"That doesn't mean I don't want you to tell Me," He answered. "It's called prayer."

She thought about that. "I thought prayer was when you ask for stuff."

"It can be. Or it can be when you just want to sit and visit with Me. That's My favorite kind of prayer, because it means you just want to spend time with Me."

She sat quietly and considered that. "I do want to spend time with You," she admitted. "As much time as You'll let me spend."

"We'll be together for eternity," He answered.

"Because of Jesus?" She looked upward, checking to make sure she had that right. It was what she truly believed and that was Who she prayed to, when she had knelt at the mourner's bench.

"Yes. Because of my Son."

"Jesus saved me," she mused, more to herself than to Father.

"Yes."

"You said You're my Father." She looked up with a question in her eyes. "But You said Jesus is Your Son."

"Yes."

"But if Jesus is the One who saved me, how come He's not the One here, now?"

"Why do you think He's not?"

"Because You said You are my Father."

"Yes. You need a Father. I Am who you need."

She pondered that.

"When will I know when it's Jesus talking to me, or when it's You?" she wondered out loud.

He assured her. "My Son and I are One."

"And the Holy Spirit?" she asked, remembering something she heard Pastor Fred say from the pulpit.

"Yes. Your life is hidden with My Son, in Me, and you are sealed by My Spirit, until the day of your redemption."

"What happens after that?" Meredith didn't mean to continue to ask questions but she didn't seem to be able to stop, once she got started, especially if Father was willing to answer them.

"You will be changed. Your mortal body will put on immortality and you will forever be with Me. My Spirit seals you now, and until that day."

Meredith's mind traveled in so many directions at once, that it began to overwhelm her. She thought miserably about her mortal body that had been ravaged and plundered by her own sin, and old tears began to reform.

"Your little one is safe with Me," Father whispered.

She began crying in earnest, not out of shame, but out of gratitude. "Thank you, Father. I love You so much!" she declared and He breathed through a gentle breeze, lifting her hair and stroking her face with a ray of warm sun.

"I love you, too."

They sat together in silence for a while, the only sound coming from the singing waters, and birds, and the dancing grasses, before her Father spoke again.

"You will not always hear Me so clearly, as you are hearing Me now."

She felt a sense of panic grip her heart and laid her hand over it. "Are You leaving? Miss Marcie said You would never leave me."

"I never will."

"Then, are You going to stop talking to me?" Fresh tears began to run down her cheeks.

"No. That is not what I said, child. I said you would not always hear Me so clearly. This is a special season and there will be others, but there will also be times when you will not yield yourself to Me as completely as you are, today. My voice will seem far away and at times, you will forget to listen. That is why it is important for you to open your mother's Bible and see it as more than just a keepsake. You will always find Me in its pages and, as you grow and mature in Me, sometimes it will be the only way you'll hear My voice. But if you search for Me, you will find Me, if you search with your whole heart."

Meredith couldn't remember having ever spent Thanksgiving with a real family, before. She must have had something like Thanksgiving with her mother, but she had no memory of any holidays with her, except for one Christmas and even that was a sad, distant recollection, incomplete and elusive.

She sat at the table now with the Blake family and couldn't keep the happiness out of her pretty eyes. Miss Marcie flashed her a sweet smile before Pastor Fred instructed them, with his customary "Let's bow."

Miss Marcie held one of her hands and her little Carlyn had hold of the other. They were all linked together, something they didn't normally do, but today, it made the holiday all the more special.

"Father, we sure can't thank You enough for sendin' us little Merry," Pastor Fred began, in a voice cracked with sentiment. She felt a rush of emotion and both Miss Marcie and Carlyn gave her fingers a little squeeze.

"We didn't even know we had any room left in our old hearts to love another daughter, especially after You gave us our beautiful Carlyn, but I reckon You've stretched our hearts and they're full again. We just pray that we care for her the way You want and that she continues to grow into the woman of God that You've always known she would become.

"We sure thank You, Lord, for blessin' us with this home, this land, these bounties You've placed on our table. Thank you for sweet Miss Marcie and her generous heart and thank You for always lookin' out for Your children with such love and tender mercies. Amen."

"Amen," Miss Marcie echoed softly.

Meredith picked up her napkin and began mopping her eyes. "I knew you'd make me cry!" she accused, twisting her mouth into a grin and flapping the napkin at Pastor Fred.

He laughed heartily and reached for the serving knife and fork to began slicing the turkey before passing it around. "It don't take much, honey. I could use you to water Miss Marcie's roses!"

$\mathcal{E}mma$ Russell looked up with a smile, as the jangling bell attached to her door rang out now, to let her know a customer was coming in. Her eyes lit up with welcome as Meredith and Carlyn greeted her.

"I bet I know why you're here!" she exclaimed, looking down at Carlyn with a teasing laugh. "You've come for your mama's birthday cake!"

"Yes, ma'am," Carlyn admitted, climbing up on a stool by the counter and looking around to see if it was nearby.

"I have it back in the kitchen. Just give me a minute, girls, and I'll bring it right out."

Emma Russell was a member of the Blake's church and ran her business out of her home, which was just down the road from the church house. She had a little trailer house set up next to her residence that served as her bakery, and she was called on by practically everyone for miles, who needed anything baked and decorated for a special occasion.

Meredith looked around at all the beautifully ornate confections and was particularly impressed with a wedding cake at the far end of the counter. It was one of the most elaborate creations she'd ever seen, and certainly rivaled anything at any of the high end shops in New Orleans. She was still examining it closely when Sister Russell came back in carrying a large cake box.

"It's just a decoy," she laughed, nodding toward the wedding cake. "The decorations and fondant are real, but the cake itself is Styrofoam."

Meredith opened her eyes wide, with a comical expression. "I'm glad I didn't try to sneak any!"

She laughed and set the cake box down carefully, motioning for Carlyn to pay attention, as she raised the lid. Meredith leaned over to look and they both drew in their breaths.

Sister Russell had designed the entire cake to resemble a woven basket and the top was overflowing with Miss Marcie's favorite flower, purple wisteria, and babies breath.

Meredith looked up at her in disbelief. "Sister Russell, those can't be real flowers in December!"

She grinned, pleased that the beautiful young woman even thought they might be. "They're sugar flowers."

"Oh, my goodness," Meredith whispered, as she and Carlyn traded huge smiles. "Miss Marcie is not gonna let anyone cut into this cake!"

Emma Russell laughed with delight. "Once she makes sure someone takes a few pictures, I think she'll be okay with it."

Meredith began to dig into her purse but she stopped her. "Oh no, sweetheart, not when I make anything for Pastor and Miss Marcie! They do so much for me and it's an honor for me to do anything I can for them."

Meredith pursed her lips in a little pout. "Pastor Fred said you'd say that, but he told me to try, anyway."

"I bet he did!" Sister Russell grinned. "Tell him he knows better."

The girls thanked her and carefully placed the cake in the backseat floorboard of Meredith's car, after Sister Russell advised that it would move less there than anywhere else in the car. Just to be sure, she packed some leftover Styrofoam chunks around the box, to keep it from sliding.

Pastor Fred had used Miss Marcie's birthday as an excuse to drive her up to Monroe earlier that day for a nice lunch, "just the two of us", as he put it, while Meredith and Carlyn collected the cake and did a few last minute things before they returned.

Once they had the cake safely inside and centered on the kitchen table, resting on a vintage cut-crystal cake stand that Emma Russell loaned them, Meredith laid a few silk wisteria flowers all around the base of it, to imitate Sister Russell's design. They brought out some presents they had been hiding and placed them all around, without a lot of time to spare before they heard Pastor Fred's Buick coming down the dirt road.

They hurried to come around and stand in front of the table so that when Miss Marcie came in, she looked at them strangely.

"Girls, is somethin' wrong?"

They looked at each other and then back at her with innocent faces and shook their heads.

"Well, then, why are you both planted there like two shrubs..." She broke off with a suspicious grin and pointed. "You go that way, and you go the other."

They laughed and obeyed and Miss Marcie was left to just stand staring, with her hands raised up to her cheeks, and her eyes lit up like stars. "Oh, my!"

"It's a beauty!" Pastor Fred came around beside his wife, with a pleased grin on his face. "That looks just like your wisteria, Marcie."

"It sure does," she breathed. "Sister Russell made this for sure, and she outdid herself!"

Her husband agreed. "Carlyn, I hope there's some film in that camera."

"There is, Daddy, I checked," she assured him, and handed it to him.

"Let's *hope* there's some film in there, or no one's cuttin' into this cake," Miss Marcie declared, her face still reflecting her delight.

"We can't do that anyway, until we sing and you blow out the candles and make a wish," Meredith informed her.

"I don't see no candles on it."

"Right here." Meredith reached beneath one of the silk wisteria blossoms around the cake stand's base and brought out a golden number five and number four, then lifted the wicks on them. "Sister Russell said not to put them on until you had seen the cake."

She waited for Pastor Fred to take a few photos, then carefully placed the candles on the topmost blossoms, and lit them and it was soon officially time to cut the cake.

"I wondered why you didn't offer me a slice of cake back at that restaurant, when that young fella came around with the dessert menu," his wife said, fixing him with a knowing look. "I wasn't all that far off from bein' put out with you, Fred Blake!"

He laughed with delight and pulled out a seat for his birthday girl, while Meredith cut the first slice for her and then served the others.

"Well, you know what this day is also about, besides your birthday, Marcie," her husband said later, after presents had been opened and the girls had taken care of cleaning up, so that Miss Marcie could relax.

Carlyn gave Meredith an excited smile, but she didn't understand what Pastor Fred was talking about.

"Marcie's birthday is always Christmas tree cuttin' eve," he informed her, looking as excited about it as any young boy might. "If the weather is tolerable, we always go out the very next day and pick out our Christmas tree and this ol' house turns into the prettiest place you ever saw!"

Meredith smiled but without the obvious excitement that his words stirred in Carlyn. "I wouldn't know much about that," she admitted, with a little shrug.

"You don't know about Christmas trees, Merry?" Carlyn stared up at her in shock.

"I know about them," Meredith corrected, with a smile. "I've just never had one."

Carlyn continued to stare, before rushing forward to throw her arms around Meredith's waist and give her a tight hug. "Our tree is your tree, too!" she assured her, in a troubled, sweet voice.

"Yes, it is," her daddy echoed. "So that means you have to pitch in and help us, Merry. We'll all bundle up in the mornin' and pick out the prettiest one we can find and then bring it in to decorate."

Meredith reached down and patted her little Carlyn on the back before giving one of her braids a little tug. "Thank you, sweetie," she said, returning her hug.

Carlyn tapped softly on Meredith's door and she answered it with a little smile.

"I'm up, baby girl," she assured her. "I just haven't started moving around much."

"Mama's got coffee made," the little girl announced.

"I smell it!" Meredith laughed. "And I'm ready for some."

She let Carlyn lead her by the hand into the kitchen.

"I'm sorry I'm still in my robe," she apologized and Miss Marcie laughed and modeled her own robe.

"Oh, honey, we're all of us usually still in our robes when Carlyn gets all worked up, and she sure is worked up this mornin'. You'd think she'd never been back in our woods, before."

"I never have been," Meredith admitted, reaching for the pot and pouring herself a cup of coffee. "I don't guess I've even been as far back as the barn."

"Well, you picked out your favorite place in that old field early on, and that's where you stuck," Miss Marcie acknowledged, sipping her own coffee. "Carlyn, you already dragged Merry and me out before either of us was ready, so you run on down the hall and tell your daddy that if he wants any of this coffee, he better shake a leg."

"I'm up," he declared, as he came into the kitchen, stopping to grab at his little girl's nose and then show her the tip of his thumb between his two fingers, as if it were the end of her nose. "Got it," he winked and she gave him the expected "oh, Daddy" and made him laugh.

He helped himself to the coffee then shook the pot at Carlyn, getting a little giggle out of her.

"One of these days, she's gonna fool you, Fred, and take you up on that coffee," her mother warned, with a grin. "For now, I think I know what she wants, though."

She tore an envelope of hot chocolate mix open and reached for the kettle she had resting on the back of the stove.

Carlyn lightly clapped her hands and took the mug when it was offered.

"That won't put no hair on your head," her daddy teased. "But it might put some on your top lip."

Meredith sat back, cradling her coffee and watching this affectionate exchange between a father and his daughter with a blend of enjoyment and sadness. She had been thinking more and more about her own daddy, recently, although she didn't know why. It might have been because during one of her quiet moments sitting in the field with her eyes closed, she suddenly realized that she did know which river he had drowned in. Clear as bell, she heard it. "Osage". She knew she was remembering correctly, even though she couldn't remember anyone actually telling her the name of the river before.

She had sat there in the tall grass, wondering what her daddy looked like. Her mother had always told her that she looked like her father, even though Lydia Clark was so beautiful that Meredith would have been pleased if she looked like her.

She had a picture of her mother in the Bible and now, as an adult, she was able to find the resemblances between the two of them, but her mother had once declared, "My goodness, Meredith, sometimes I look at you and I see Hollis looking back at me!" It might have been his eyes, since Lydia's eyes were a beautiful sky blue and hers were only gray. Meredith had no idea that her eyes were one of her most exceptional features.

She hadn't meant to let out a sigh that could be heard but she must have, because Miss Marcie reached over from her chair and rested a gentle hand on her back. They traded a little smile and Miss Marcie let it go at that.

"Let me see if I can't throw some kinda breakfast together, real quick," she said. "We can't go trudgin' out through the pasture with nothing more in our stomachs than a little coffee sloshin' around."

It took her practically no time at all to whip up a large platter of steaming, soft pancakes and heated syrup and butter and after a blessing, everyone dug in.

"Remind me, Fred, to call Sister Russell today and thank her for the cake." Miss Marcie glanced around to see if anyone needed anything.

"I've always wondered about that," Meredith began, looking around at the others.

"About what, Merry?" Pastor Fred prompted, when she seemed to second guess asking.

"Why everyone at church is either called sister or brother," she said. "Is that from the Bible?"

"No, honey, that's not a command or even a doctrine," Pastor Fred answered, with a kind smile. "Although Jesus did say 'whoever does My Father's will is My brother and sister and mother'. But He wasn't definin' natural brotherhood, He was speakin' about spiritual connections.

"We're all brothers and sisters in the Lord, but it's really a sign of affection, not a doctrinal practice. And, as far as I've ever been able to tell, it's mostly a southern thing. Marcie and I have visited a few churches up north and I don't remember hearin' any of them callin' each other brother and sister."

"It's just a church family thing," his wife agreed, "but it's perfectly fine for you to say mister or missus and no one would bat an eye."

Meredith nodded and added this to the list of things she was learning, and finished her breakfast more quickly when she saw that Carlyn was done and was beginning to fidget.

They were soon all bundled up and making their way across the field and it was all Meredith could do to not excuse herself and run over to the branch to see if Father was there, even though He'd told her in one of their chats that He was everywhere she went. Still, it was their special place, as far as Meredith was concerned.

She stayed with the group and began to be more interested in their mission as they neared the barn where she had never yet gone. They stopped and looked inside it while Pastor Fred took a saw down off a hook, then waited while he unlocked a large metal gate to let them move on into the woods.

Meredith stopped and stared all around. The tall pine trees all rose majestically in front of her and the smell here was intoxicating.

Miss Marcie observed her reaction. "Now, you'll have to come back out here in the spring, Merry, and see the dogwoods and redbuds bloomin'. This place can't even be described when all the color pops in these woods!"

"Oh, I can't wait," she replied, her eyes taking in every new thing around her. She looked back toward the house. "How many acres is your property?"

"Sixty-seven acres," Miss Marcie said, "but most of it is these woods. All the fields together with our yard are only about sixteen, I reckon. The trees all around the road and our driveway are part of it. It all sort of wraps around us."

"How long have you had it?" Meredith stood still, taking it all in.

"My goodness, it was Fred's daddy's and his, before him. A long time, I guess."

"I've had my eye on a nice little red cedar back here," Pastor Fred said back over his shoulder, as he led their party through the towering pines and oaks.

"How little is it, Daddy?" Carlyn was concerned and he laughed.

"Don't you worry, Carlyn Darlin'. It's as tall as your ol' daddy is."

Her face lit up and she looked back at Meredith with an eager grin.

"Children are always excited about Christmas, I guess," she commented softly.

"Well, grownups can be, as well," Miss Marcie replied. "But I reckon it all depends on what a person is expectin' outta Christmas."

Meredith knew there was more to her simple statement than Miss Marcie gave away, but as frank and as blunt as she could be, Marcie Blake was also just as prone to let the meanings of some of her remarks reveal themselves in their own time.

Carlyn had dashed on ahead of them and now came running back, her green eyes brilliant with happiness. "I saw it, Mama!   It's the one!   Daddy found a good one!"

Miss Marcie looked on up ahead and saw her husband waiting for them with a joyful smile on his face as he watched his little girl's glee.

"Carlyn says you found it."

"The good Lord planted it a long while back, just for that look on our little girl's face, today," he returned, in his whimsical way.

Meredith thought about his words and looked back across the property toward the place where the little branch ran, wild and free, and where the tall grasses happily waved at her from a great distance, and a sweetness rested on her face. Somehow, she knew that Father had prepared all of it long ago, knowing that a frightened and abused young woman would stumble into its refuge and find Him waiting there.

$\mathcal{M}iss$ Marcie was right, Meredith decided. This place couldn't even be described. Her eyes roamed all across the tree line at the back of the field and were treated to the pink and white dogwood blossoms, silver bells, and redbuds. Yellow forsythia leaped out from among the palette, and a wealth of wild violets and butterweed insisted on washing the ground with color, particularly alongside the branch, where they hugged its banks with their beauty. She stood for a long while, being treated to the sights and sounds and scents of the meadows, then drew in a deep breath of appreciation.

Christmas had come and gone, the first one that Meredith could remember ever being a part of, since her aunt and uncle always celebrated by working, traveling or drinking. This Christmas had been a time of spiritual beauty, because the Blake family had focused their celebration of the holiday around the birth of their Savior.

The most poignant moment of the day had been when little Carlyn had come shyly into the living room, packing her daddy's guitar, which was almost bigger than she was, and handed Meredith a sheet of paper with words the child had penned herself. Meredith had looked down at the large, rounded letters, hardly able to read them, as her eyes misted over when she heard Carlyn say, "I wrote a song for your present, Merry."

Meredith had listened as Carlyn strummed the same three chords over and over, singing in her clear, sweet voice. She noted that the meter was correct and that her words rhymed in a way that made sense, but what fully arrested her attention was that the child had chosen to write a song about a girl who found love in a new home with a new family and was safe in her Father's arms. She had titled the song "In Father's Field".

Of course, Meredith had broken down in tears and gathered little Carlyn onto her lap for a tight hug and words of praise, recognizing her talent and assuring her that she should continue to write songs, because God had given music to her to be used for Him and to bless others.

That had been as much a Christmas gift to Carlyn as anything that had been wrapped for her to open, and she responded with a smile that Meredith would never lose sight of, in the years to come.

Meredith had allowed her thoughts to travel back to that sweet Christmas day and stood silent now, in the March breezes, somehow sensing that time was moving too quickly. She didn't understand where this feeling was coming from, but she could feel it steadily encroaching.

She turned at the sound of trampling through the brush and half expected Father, but saw Carlyn making her way toward her with a happy grin.

"Daddy says to ask you if you want anything special planted in the garden." Carlyn delivered the message, then added in her little teasing way, "I told him I thought you'd like watermelons, but he said you prob'ly want radishes."

She giggled and Meredith giggled with her. "I don't even know what radishes are for, except maybe for salads, but I've never put them in one. I agree with you, baby girl. Let's go tell him we want watermelons."

She let her little sidekick lead her back to the yard by one hand and was again aware of a sad feeling that her days with this sweet little girl couldn't possibly last forever. Meredith resisted that thought and applied herself to listening to every word Carlyn was saying, as if she needed to paste them in some sort of scrapbook in her heart.

"How many rows of radishes do you need, Merry?" Pastor Blake looked up from his hoeing and flashed her a bright smile.

"I think just enough for you and Miss Marcie," she returned with a little grin. "I'm good. But Carlyn wants two rows of watermelons."

"Oh, *Carlyn* does!" He belted out a laugh and went back to digging pockets into the soil he'd tilled the day before, then stopped.

"Look here, Carlyn Darlin', at this big ol' earthworm!" She wrinkled her nose and stepped back and he picked it up and held it out. "You know what that means, don't cha, honey? The fish are bitin'."

Meredith brightened up when she heard that. She had been hoping they'd be able to fish more than they had.

Miss Marcie came out of the back door with a laundry basket of wet sheets and looked over at them with a smile. "If they're bitin', Fred Blake, then how come you're not catchin' 'em?"

Meredith came over to help Miss Marcie manage the sheets and keep them from touching the ground, while she draped them over the clothes line and secured them with the wooden pegs. She used her dryer for most things, but Miss Marcie loved the way sheets smelled when they had been drying out in the sun.

Pastor Blake leaned on his hoe and looked around at the sky. "That's a good question, Marcie. I 'spect the answer is that you already told me to get these seeds in the ground. Fishin' might have to wait until this afternoon."

Miss Marcie rested one hand on her hip and scanned the sky, herself. "I reckon they'll still be hungry later, and maybe I can go along too, by then. It won't take these sheets long to dry."

She looked down at her baby girl with a little smile. "Guess what your mama found this mornin', Carly."

Carlyn looked up expectantly and waited.

"You don't want to try and guess?" Miss Marcie laughed. "Because, if you think about it, I bet you could."

Carlyn looked all around and everyone could see her little mind working to come up with a guess. Finally, she let out a sigh and shook her head. "I can't think, Mama."

"Come on over here, and I'll show you. You come too, Merry, and see what we got."

Miss Marcie led the way around and behind the shed where Pastor Blake usually kept his lawn mower and yard tools and slightly pulled back a small piece of plywood that was leaning against it. She put in her hand and pulled out a tiny, fuzzy white ball of fur and Carlyn gave a little laugh and clapped her hands, before holding them out to take the kitten.

"We got three more in here, Merry," she announced, and set the piece of plywood over to one side.

Meredith knelt down and picked up a tiny black one, with white markings on its chest. "It looks like he's wearing a little tuxedo," she said, giving him a gentle kiss and holding him next to her cheek.

"They're at least a few days old, I'm guessin', because their little eyes is open," Miss Marcie speculated. "The mama cat never let on like she'd had them. I knew she was fixin' to, at any time, but she didn't give me no clues, like our other mama cat did.

"Fred, we gotta get Doc McNeil to fix her, as soon as she's ready, 'cause this ain't no cat farm," she stated firmly, but not without still wearing her little smile.

Merry traded her kitten for Carlyn's little white one and then the other black and white kitten and the solid black one seemed to need equal time, before Miss Marcie brought the piece of wood back over.

"That mama cat'll only put up with so much, before she starts fussin' at us, girls. I reckon we outta put 'em back where she left 'em."

They were handed back to Miss Marcie obediently, but reluctantly, and shielded once more behind the plywood.

Pastor Fred came over and quietly studied their makeshift home for a moment. "Marcie, let's bring these little fellas onto the screen porch for a spell, until they're big enough to not be so attractive to snakes and hawks."

She crossed her arms and thought about it. "I reckon we can put the mama in there with 'em, but she can't keep running in and out, tearin' up my screen."

"Let's just set her up with a litter box and see how she does," the kindhearted old pastor suggested. "That way, she'll be easy to catch when it's time for Doc McNeil to spay her."

The garden was put on hold for a short while, until all the kittens were relocated to the safety of the screened back porch and their mother was placed inside to care for them.

"Well, we'll have to get some cat litter, at some point," Pastor Fred decided, "but this pottin' soil will work in her box, for now."

Between food and water, the cow rug and some old ticking fabric that had been retired and was supposed to have already made it out to the burn barrel, Mama Cat and her babies had been made very comfortable and were living in, as Miss Marcie put it, "tall cotton".

Pastor Fred had disappeared into his shed and now came out with a roll of half-inch grid rabbit wire and a large staple gun. "I'm gonna wrap this around the outside of the porch, from the railin' on down, Marcie. It'll save your screen and I 'spect it'll discourage anything from trying to force its way in here. We can take it down, once these little fellas are out and about."

She nodded in approval, then picked up her empty laundry basket. "I'll be out in a minute, to help you finish your gardenin', Fred. Then I'll put us all a picnic lunch together and we can go see about all them hungry fish you been goin' on about. Maybe Carlyn can rustle up some more worms."

It took her a minute, but Carlyn finally realized she was joking. It was her daddy's burst of laughter that gave it away.

⚬⚬⚬

Normally, Carlyn shied away from leaving the truck bed when her parents were fishing, because she didn't enjoy seeing the fish get caught, but Meredith liked to fish, so that went a long way toward convincing her to hop down and join them.

Miss Marcie stopped her and called Meredith over as well, and made them stand still while she sprayed their feet and legs with tick repellant. "It's the season," she explained and turned to make sure her husband was armed against the little parasites, as well.

"Want me to rig you up a pole, Carly?" her dad asked with a grin, after his wife was satisfied that he smelled as badly as the rest of them.

"No, sir," she answered. "I'm just watchin' y'all."

"Well, if you watch us fish, you might end up watchin' us catch 'em, so don't say your old daddy didn't warn you," he laughed.

She grinned and came over to stand next to Meredith, which was where anyone usually found her, when she wasn't in school. Meredith smiled down at her.

"You're sure you don't want to try?"

Carlyn shook her head and grinned shyly. She just wasn't ready.

"Is it going to bother you, if I catch a fish?" Meredith waiting before casting, and Carlyn shook her head again.

"No, I want you to have fun."

She reached over and lightly tugged at the child's golden brown braid. "Thank you, sweet girl."

She had to laugh when Carlyn's eyes opened wide and she grabbed her nose, as Meredith put the blood bait on her hook.

The first time Meredith landed a catfish, Carlyn closed her eyes but by the time several fish had been caught, she had forgotten to not look and had become interested.

Pastor Fred noticed, but kept his teasing to a minimum, since he wanted her to come to enjoy fishing as much as they did.

They finally had what Miss Marcie called "a right good mess" and Pastor Fred stowed them into the back of his truck, while his wife made sure everyone took a wet towel out of the trash bag and passed the soap around to clean their hands.

The lawn chairs were unfolded, and ham and cheese sandwiches, and chips were set out on the tailgate, along with a metal cooler of cold sweet tea.

This was Carlyn's favorite part of these outings, just sitting and eating her lunch, and listening to her family laugh and talk. Today was no exception.

The conversation was light and humorous and carefree but Pastor Fred and Miss Marcie noticed that Meredith grew silent after a while, and appeared to have stopped listening.

"Are you alright, darlin'?" Miss Marcie asked. "You look like you're a million miles away."

Meredith bit her lip and stared out at the waters of Castor Creek and nodded, but it was easy to see that she had suddenly become emotional.

Carlyn jumped up and ran around to kneel by her chair and take her hand. "Did you want to keep fishing, Merry? We don't have to stop. I like fishing now, I promise!"

In spite of what was going on inside of her, Meredith had to laugh, even as tears had begun to splash down her cheeks.

"No, baby girl, I've fished enough for today, but thank you." She patted her lap and Carlyn hopped up and settled against her, resting her head on Meredith's shoulder.

Pastor Fred and Miss Marcie looked at each other with sad understanding passing between them. They had already determined that Meredith was going through some sort of transition, although she, herself, hadn't seemed to be aware of it, until today.

Miss Marcie had tucked her little girl in and heard her prayers, instructing her not to read too long, since tomorrow morning was church. She gave her a kiss on her forehead, then headed down the hall to her own room, stopping as she realized that Meredith's light was still on.

She tapped lightly and waited for her response before letting herself in.

Meredith smiled up at her from where she was sitting on her bedside. She was still dressed and had made no move to go to bed, even though she had excused herself after supper, with that explanation.

Miss Marcie returned her smile and came over to sit down beside her.

"Do you even know what's wrong, little lamb?" she asked, glancing over at her with kind eyes.

Meredith remembered her first night in this room, when Miss Marcie called her "little lamb" and informed her that she saw more than she let on, and she smiled down at the floor.

"No, I really don't," she answered quietly. "I've just been feeling a sadness off and on, all day." She looked over at Miss Marcie, who could see the signs of fresh tears. "I keep trying to push it away, but it keeps coming back."

Miss Marcie sat quietly for a moment, absently studying the pattern of the rug by Meredith's bed. "Are you sure you're supposed to push it away, honey?"

Meredith seemed surprised. "I mean... it doesn't feel like a good thing." She hung her head. "I don't like the way it feels."

Miss Marcie let out a heavy sigh before asking the question she'd been avoiding. "Does it feel like goodbye, Merry?"

Meredith no longer blinked back her tears, but let them rain down her face, as she leaned her head over onto Miss Marcie's shoulder and quietly sobbed, then nodded.

"Do I have to go?" she asked, brokenly.

"Not if Fred and I have any say in it," the pastor's wife was quick to reply, wrapping her arms around her, and then stroking her hair with a motherly hand. "But we have to find out, darlin', if all this is God's doin'. If it is, we can't meddle with it. Of course, we hope it's not, because that way, you could stay with us forever, and that's what we wish for. If anyone in this world was ever meant to come be a part of this family, it's you."

She stopped and looked more closely at Meredith's tear-streaked face. "Honey, do you remember God sayin' anything specific to you, right before you started feelin' all this?"

"No, but..." She hesitated, then bent forward and reached under her bed, pulling out the leather satchel.

Miss Marcie looked at it curiously and watched while Meredith undid the buckle and carefully slid the old Bible out.

"My mother gave it to me before she died," she explained. "Father said I would need to start reading it, so I have been, but I really haven't known where to start. But lately, it keeps opening to this verse. This morning, I went ahead and bookmarked it, but I really didn't need to."

She found the section where she had placed the little bookmark Carlyn had made for her and put in her Christmas stocking, and lifted it up for Marcie Blake to read.

She noted that the passage was in Jeremiah then read aloud, *"Oh, Lord, I know the way of a man is not in himself; it is not in man who walks, to direct his own steps."* She closed the Bible and laid it back into Meredith's hands.

"What do you think this is sayin' to you, Merry?"

She shook her head and stared down at the floor and neither woman spoke for a while. Finally, she made herself say it.

"I think it's saying that the time will come, when I have to go out on my own and say goodbye." She looked up at Marcie Blake with eyes that broke the old woman's heart. "And that will hurt me more than I can even say.

"I was so afraid when I came here. I almost slipped out after everyone had gone to bed, that first night, but I kept remembering that you asked me not to do that, and you had all been so kind. I couldn't go through with it and it was true what you said, the next morning. Even if I'd gotten in my car, I had no idea where to drive it.

"I was alone. I've always been alone, since my mother died, until I came here."

"What about your aunt and uncle, Merry? Did you feel alone there, too?

"I ran away from there, to New Orleans, when I was sixteen."

Miss Marcie drew in her breath quietly. She had known that Meredith had been singing in New Orleans but she had no idea she had run away to go there. Her silent question hung in the air between them.

"My uncle tried..." Meredith halted. "They both were drunks, but he was the one I was afraid of. He was always looking at me, and one night, he came in my room."

Miss Marcie took her hand and shook her head. "I think I'll spare you the rest of that, sweetie. It's not too hard to follow, but it prob'ly is too hard for you to talk about."

"Miss Marcie..." Meredith gave her a look of pleading. "This is the only place I've ever felt safe. Why would Father do this to me?"

Just as she had done when they both knelt at the mourner's bench, Miss Marcie put an arm around her and helped her cry.

Chapter Eleven

Pastor Fred sat at the kitchen table, nursing the cup of coffee his wife had given him, seemingly lost in thought. The telephone had rung earlier and he'd picked it up.

Miss Marcie had just assumed it was someone from the church and had gone on into the kitchen to get breakfast ready. She wished now that she'd paid more attention to the call, because her husband had been unusually quiet, since he'd hung the phone up.

Meredith came in with Carlyn in tow, and made her way over to the coffee pot. She turned and looked back at Pastor Fred, waiting for him to joke with Carlyn and offer her some coffee, but he hadn't seemed to notice them.

He did now, though. "Carly, didn't you tell me you wanted to make some extra spendin' money, once school was out for the summer?"

"Yes, sir!" She came over, eager for her assignment. She'd been wanting her own guitar, something smaller than her father's, and she was hoping to be able to put enough money into her piggybank to buy it before school started again. Of course, she had a birthday coming in August, and maybe, if she hadn't made enough money by then, her parents might help her with the rest, but she wanted to earn as much of it as she could.

"I seem to remember you bein' pretty handy with a paintbrush," her daddy remarked, and she smiled broadly. She loved painting!

"After breakfast, I'll go out with you and set you up and get you started. I'd like you to paint that ol' front gate, both sides, and I'll pay you cash, when you're done. Think you can handle that?"

She nodded, excitement in her eyes, but her mother stood looking at Fred Blake with suspicion in hers. That gate had been painted less than a year ago, and it still looked fresh. He glanced up to find her reading him and looked back down at his coffee.

"I just made some biscuits and egg gravy, this mornin', and fried up some sausage," Miss Marcie said. "But I reckon that'll be enough get us all started."

Meredith pulled the plates down out of the cabinet and Carlyn tore off several sheets of paper towels and grabbed some forks. Breakfast was soon on the table and Pastor Fred offered up thanks.

It was a quieter meal than normal, although Pastor Fred did make the occasional effort to get a grin out of his little girl. He finally pushed up from his chair and Carlyn hurried to join him.

"Let me get my shoes on, Daddy," she called out, as she made her way back to her room.

Fred Blake brought his cup and plate to the sink and glanced over at his wife, who was running enough hot water to wash up the breakfast dishes.

"Y'all don't run off," he said to her softly, looking back at Meredith, who was collecting cups and forks.

Carlyn had slipped into her shoes and reappeared almost instantly and her father smiled down at her.

"Now, I don't want you to rush through this job, baby girl. I want you to take your time and try not to get too much paint on them hinges. Then just step back and see if you missed anything and maybe do a little touch up. The scriptures say that the laborer is worthy of his hire, and if you do a good job, you will be too, honey."

She nodded soberly and followed her daddy out to gather everything she would need for the job.

Miss Marcie usually turned down offers to help clean up after breakfast but she let Meredith help her now, in order to keep her from heading out to the fields, since Pastor Blake had requested that they not run off.

She soon heard him come back in the front door and saw him standing, looking through the screen at Carlyn, then he turned around and met her eyes, before coming back to sit down at the kitchen table.

"Marcie, you and Merry come sit down," he said.

Meredith looked at him with a puzzled expression. Pastor Fred had been unusually stoic this morning and she felt his request had something to do with it.

She looked over at Miss Marcie and the two of them came and sat down and waited.

Pastor Fred reached over and began toying with the edge of a doily that had been put back on the center of the table after breakfast.

"I gave little Carly somethin' to do," he began, "to keep her from hearin' and gettin' upset." He heaved out a sigh and prepared to get on with it.

"I had a phone call this mornin', pretty early," he finally said. He lifted his eyes and rested them on Meredith's confused expression. "It was from the sheriff's office."

Pastor Fred had been silently praying for God to help him with this, and now he leaned back in his chair to cross his arms and continue.

"Merry, there's an attorney in St. Louis who's lookin' for you."

Alarm immediately registered on her beautiful face and she lifted a hand to her throat.

"They can't make me go back there, can they?" she whispered to Miss Marcie. "I'm not a minor."

"It's not about that," Pastor Fred cut in gently. He reached over gave her a little pat on her arm. "It's nothin' to be afraid of, honey, but it's somethin' you need to know."

He reached into his shirt pocket and pulled out a scrap of paper he had written some things on, but simply held onto it, while he prompted himself to finish.

"Your aunt and uncle are both dead, Merry."

She just blinked and stared.

"Apparently, your uncle died some time ago, but your aunt was killed in a car crash fairly recently. I'm sorry," he was quick to add.

Meredith looked down at her hands, wondering how she was supposed to feel about this. It did occur to her that it would be a tragic thing if her uncle and aunt had gone into eternity unprepared to meet God, and she suspected that this was probably the case but, beyond that, she felt nothing. She simply nodded.

"It don't end there," Fred Blake added, leaning onto his forearms and giving her a direct look. "You have an inheritance, Merry."

She raised her eyes to his with a blank expression, not really registering what he was saying.

"I guess your aunt and uncle must have been fairly well off, accordin' to what's been said."

She nodded. "Insurance and real estate, so I guess so. I think they had some properties and investments."

"From what I've been told, you are what's called the 'heir apparent'. I don't understand everything about that, except that, in your case, you seem to be the only heir, at all. I take it your aunt and uncle had no children?"

She shook her head. "They never did."

"Well, this attorney has been doin' what they call 'due diligence' and I reckon he'll be the one to tell you what trail he followed to find you, but I do know that he focused on this state. Someone up there must have known which way you was headed, when you ran off. The sheriff's offices in every parish seat, along with metro police stations were notified.

"Of course, Buck Weed, at the sheriff's office, knew that you was stayin' out here, so he decided to call me, instead of drivin' out and gettin' everyone upset, and I told him I appreciated that."

They all sat silent for a moment, before Meredith slipped a hand up to wipe a few tears from the corners of her eyes.

"I don't want it," she whispered.

"I figured you'd say that." The pastor smiled sadly down at the table, then raised his eyes. "But, Merry, you need to spend some time prayin' about it. The attorney has been notified that you've been located and he's been told that you'll make contact with him within a week. Buck took care of lettin' him know, and I 'spect he'll be fine with that. Of course, I don't know anything about his time frame or any of that, but if anything is pressin' at this point, I 'spect he'll reach out to Buck. He didn't give him our name or number. Buck's a good friend."

Meredith looked over at Miss Marcie, with a sad, teary smile. "Remember, I said?"

She nodded. "I know you did, sweetie. It's pretty clear that God's been preparin' you for some kinda change. That's why you need to listen to Pastor now, and not just make your mind up without talkin' to the Lord about all this. If you go by your feelin's, that might be a mistake."

"But I love this life, here," Meredith said quietly.

"Darlin', all you'll be doin' is findin' out more about your situation," Miss Marcie pointed out. "No one's askin' you to move out, we're just sayin' that you need to pray and find out what the Lord wants you to do. If He wants you to stay here and let all that go, then we're mor'n happy about that. It's like I said, honey. If anyone in this world was ever meant to come be a part of this family, it's you.

"But some things are for a lifetime and some things are just for a season, and you need to know which one is true about your time here. You can't just choose which one you want it to be. You hafta let the Lord tell you. Remember that verse," she reminded gently.

Meredith nodded then looked up at Pastor Fred with tears still finding their way down her face. "Can we just send an address and ask for something in writing?"

"That's a good idea, Merry, and we'll just use the church's post office box for that," Pastor Fred agreed. "I think that's more than fair, for that attorney to spell everything out before you just head off to St. Louis, or anywhere else. I'll give Buck a call back and we'll ask for that."

Meredith wiped her face again and gave them both a relieved smile. "Is it okay if I go watch Carlyn paint?"

They both grinned at her and Miss Marcie stood up and waved her toward the front yard. "Go on, sweetie. I reckon she'll be glad for your company."

"But don't help her, Merry," Carlyn's daddy admonished. "She has to do the work herself. She knows that."

He watched her go with a faint smile that soon faded away and stood up to look at his wife with sad eyes. "I 'spect she'll end up goin', Marcie."

"I 'spect she will."

She made her way over to the sink, but just stood there with her head down, as her shoulders began to shake. Her husband came over and put an arm around her.

"Alright, darlin'. You head on back to our room and get all that cryin' done before Carlyn comes runnin' back in here. You and me have to keep the peace of God on our faces today, for both those girls."

Meredith walked slowly back from the fields where she'd been for the past few hours, ever since reading the letter that arrived today from the attorney's office and quietly excusing herself.

Carlyn had hopped up out of her chair to run after her, but her mother called her back to come help her feed the kittens, then her daddy asked her to ride into town with him to pick up some cornmeal and run a few errands.

Now, as she neared the yard, Meredith turned back to gaze at the tall grasses and the branch and her special hiding place where she and Father had spent so much time getting to know each other.

She had no way of knowing if she'd ever meet Him out in the field again, because when He'd talked with her today, He asked her to be obedient and to trust Him, and it was with a heavy heart that she knew she must leave this paradise behind and once again, travel toward the unknown. Meredith had cried many tears; some of them were bitter and some angry but her last ones had been tears of repentance and surrender. It was then that she felt Father's hand on her and His peace washed over her.

Now, her eyes slowly roamed all over the vast fields and trees and barn and the faintest smile rested on her lips. Her heart began to fill up with thankfulness and a deep and abiding love for this simple, yet wonderful family who had taken her in, a stranger, and adopted her as their own.

She turned back, as the sound of Pastor Fred's old pickup truck came rumbling down the dirt road. As it rounded the circle and stopped, Carlyn threw open the door and came running, her long braids flying up and down.

She threw her arms around her big sister's waist and told her all about the baby deer someone had with them at the feed store and how it had eaten corn from her hand.

Meredith smiled at the child's animated story and listened with a twinge of sadness, realizing how much love hurt, and hoping it was worth the pain.

Chapter Twelve

Meredith stood, when the receptionist let her know that the attorney was ready to see her. She returned her smile and followed her in.

Malcomb Laird rose and greeted her with an introduction and a handclasp. He gestured toward a chair and she quietly took a seat.

The elderly Mr. Laird had been the Wickham's attorney for many years and, although he knew that the daughter of Phyllis Wickham's late sister had been living with them, he hadn't been prepared for this beautiful and poised young woman, now sitting in his office. He'd supposed, when she had been described to him as a runaway, that he would be meeting with some sullen, gum-popping girl with a sense of entitlement and a morbid glee that her aunt and uncle were dead and gone, leaving the way clear for her to simply take what was rightfully hers.

He sat back in his chair and regarded her with a professional detachment, but was unable to hide his relief.

"Miss Clark, can I get you anything? Something to drink, perhaps?"

"No, thank you," Meredith declined with a smile, and patiently waited.

"I'm sure you've figured this out yourself, but it was a high school chum of yours who saw the personal ad looking for you and contacted my office. You must have told her your plans, because she was rather certain that you had taken a bus from St. Louis to New Orleans."

Meredith furrowed her brow and tried to remember who she would have shared that information with. She did have some vague memory of crying in the bathroom at school once, after her uncle had begun looking at her inappropriately, and blurting out that if he ever touched her, she would run away, but she certainly didn't remember saying anything about going to New Orleans, although that had been her intention. Apparently, she'd said more to the girls in the bathroom that day than she realized.

"No matter, I suppose," the attorney said, seeing her struggle to place the schoolmate. "The fortunate thing is that she was correct and it at least took our search to the right state and made things much easier. I must tell you, without much to go on, you were the proverbial needle in the haystack. It was only fate, I suppose, that she saw the personal ad and responded."

Meredith made no comment, but gave him another quiet smile.

"Miss Clark..." he leaned forward onto his elbows and gave her a searching look. "Do you have any idea of the size of the Wickham's estate?"

"No, sir," she said. "I remember their house was nice, but I never thought about it, I suppose."

He settled back into his chair and regarded her quietly. "It was your Aunt Phyllis who changed the will, leaving everything to you."

Meredith appeared startled and her surprise was genuine. "When did she do that?"

"Not long after your uncle died, although she had contacted me right after you ran away, and instructed me that, in the event of her pre-deceasing her husband, any and all of her personal assets were to go to you. Of course, the last will makes that one redundant."

She sat in silence and just shook her head. She'd always believed that her aunt had no more use for her than anyone else. There was no interaction between them, hardly any communication and certainly no affection. Meredith had never sensed anything from her but resentment.

Mr. Laird seemed to read her thoughts and broke into them with quiet words. "She was very sorry, Miss Clark."

"Sorry?" She lifted her eyes to him in confusion.

"She knew." He waited silently to see if he would have to spell it out, hoping that he wouldn't. Now, Meredith simply nodded, and he relaxed.

"After your uncle died, she came to see me and that's when she drew up a will stating that everything in its entirety was to be left to you. She was very firm about it. It is, as I indicated in the letter, a sizable estate."

Meredith continued to amaze the old attorney by not asking how much she was inheriting. She simply sat and listened, almost as if it had still not occurred to her that she controlled the entire Wickham fortune and could do with it as she pleased.

"Miss Clark, the Wickham estate, including their home, stocks and bonds, investment properties, real estate, vacation properties, bank accounts and miscellaneous items, such as jewelry, antiques, paintings and the like are valued in excess of almost two million dollars, net worth."

She continued to rest her gaze on him, as if she didn't realize he was done.

"Do you have any questions about any of this, as far as the property, itself?" He waited.

"I don't know the sort of questions I'm meant to ask," she stated honestly.

He nodded, completely understanding the unusual position this young woman found herself in.

"Since much of the Wickham's wealth was considered liquid and there were no debts, the estate has already gone through probate. The will is very straightforward and indisputable, having been drawn up by your aunt in my presence, here in this office, and witnessed accordingly. It's a simple matter of now transferring the estate to you."

Meredith raised her lovely eyes to his and the blush of a smile washed over her face. "I suppose simple is a relative term," she said, and the attorney laughed.

"I suppose, but in this case, most of it was seen to, proactively. Your aunt seemed to want things to be easy for you."

"I didn't know her very well," Meredith confessed, with a troubled look. "I feel badly about that. But she didn't seem to want to know me and when she drank..." She broke off, dismayed that she had let that slip, but Mr. Laird nodded in understanding.

"She did seem to do much less of that, toward the end," he said. "I hope that's some comfort."

"Mr. Laird," she said, impulsively. "Do you know if... would you have any way of knowing, or finding out, if Aunt Phyllis kept the storage fees paid where my mother's things were taken, after she died?"

"If that's the storage facility near St. Thomas, then yes, that is listed as one of the bills that one of her bank accounts pays automatically. Barring any sort of vandalism or theft, everything should still be there."

"It's been a long time, though," she said, with a sigh. "At least seven years, maybe eight."

"I see no interruption in the payments being made every month, nothing to indicate the business being sold or having changed names. If you like, I can call and make an inquiry."

"Please." She gave him a grateful smile. "My mother's old upright piano was in there. It's not fancy, or anything. But I loved it." She smiled sadly. "My mother and I sang together and before she got so sick, we sat on the piano bench together. I learned harmonies and my mother taught me to play along with her."

She flashed him a look of apology. "I don't mean to go on about it, I'm sorry. I just wondered about it."

Mr. Laird quietly marveled that this young lady could buy the most impressive concert grand in the world, but only cared about what was probably just a cheap upright. That said a lot to him about her character.

"I feel fairly confident that anything that was taken to that storage building is still there, but I do need to determine where the keys are or if there's a combination. If neither are available, then we'll have to talk to the storage owner about that. I'll see to it," he promised. "Where are you staying in St. Louis, Miss Clark?"

He slid a notepad and a pen toward her and she wrote down the details of her hotel and the number of the new phone that the Blakes absolutely would not let her leave town without buying. They had to know that she had a way to get in touch with them, if she needed them.

"I'll need to meet with you at the Wickham's primary banking institution to set up your own account and have funds transferred. After that, there are other funds and banks to approach similarly. I'm afraid you'll have to see me more often than you might like while you're here, but hopefully, it won't be a complete nuisance. I'll have my secretary call you to set that up and to give you the address and we'll just continue to work through what must seem overwhelming to you, right now. But it'll all be fine."

Mr. Laird stood with her and reached for her hand and Meredith thanked him again, before leaving. The old attorney watched her go and felt a sting of indignation at the way Don Wickham had treated such a lovely and decent young girl.

Pastor Fred signaled to his wife and daughter and held the phone up with a happy grin. They immediately knew that their Merry was on the line, and hurried over.

"Hang on, Merry, I'm tryin' to get this thing where we can all hear you." Pastor Fred put his glasses on and searched for the small square button that engaged the speakerphone and pressed it. "How 'bout that, Merry, can you still hear me? I never tried it before."

"I can!" Her laughter was heard in the room, and Miss Marcie and Carlyn both shouted their greetings, causing Meredith to laugh even more.

Pastor Fred held on to the receiver, not yet trusting the phone not to disconnect them, if he hung it up, but the connection seemed clear.

"Where are you, Merry?" Miss Marcie was still yelling, unsure of whether the phone was working both ways, as it should.

Meredith laughed again. "I'm in St. Thomas, right now. But I wanted to tell you that I'll be moving to Poplar Bluff in about a week.   I found a little cottage near the river, so I can go fishing!"

"We'll have to look that up on a map, honey," Pastor Fred informed her. "What river runs through there?"

"Black River," she replied.

"The same Black River that the Ouachita turns into?" Carlyn asked hopefully.

"I haven't been able to tell, trying to follow it on a map, sweetie, but I sure hope so. That would connect us. But I wish it was Black Bayou."

"We do too, darlin', for sure!" Miss Marcie declared. "But if it can't be, then I reckon Black River is good enough. I 'spect there's catfish swimmin' around in there, same as in the bayou."

"I sure hope so. I intend to find out." She paused for a second. "Carlyn, are the kittens grown, now?"

"They look grown, but they don't act like it," she reported. "Preacher climbs up the outside of the screen, tryin' to get back in and Mama says he's a reprobate."

"Oh, my goodness, that is so funny!" Meredith laughed heartily at Carlyn's tale of the kitten wearing the furry black suit and white collar that she had named Preacher. "You better take him to the mourner's bench, so he can repent!"

They all happily agreed and Meredith began to feel as if she were right there with them.

"I sure do miss all of you. I hope we can have some visits, soon."

"Well, for now, I 'spect we'll have to content ourselves with callin', but you just never can tell," Pastor Fred remarked, grinning at the way Miss Marcie and Carlyn brightened up. "We just might surprise you."

"Merry, I'm writing some songs!" Carlyn hurried to get this into the conversation while she could.

"Oh, I'm so glad to hear that, baby girl," she said, with both smiles and tears wrestling for dominance. "I sure wish I could hear them."

"Maybe she can record some and send them to you," Miss Marcie proposed.

"Oh, I hope so! Carlyn, you just keep on singing and writing, sweetie. You never know, maybe you and I will meet up in Nashville, Tennessee someday, and we can sing together."

Carlyn's eyes shone like stars and she clasped her hands to her mouth.

"She ain't sayin' nothin', but you outta see this girl's face. You just made her day," her daddy laughed.

Meredith grinned, able to imagine the way Carlyn's little face was shining.

"I'll be in St. Thomas a few more days, before I go down to Poplar Bluff," she told them. "This is where my mother and I lived, you know, and I have to check on her things that were left in storage. But this is a good three hours, maybe more, from Poplar Bluff, so I'll probably rent storage down there and arrange for everything to be moved.

"The Osage River is here," she let Pastor Fred know. "But I won't go fishing in it, I'll just wait until I get to Black River. You'll be able to see both rivers on a map, though."

They exchanged a little more small talk and news before Meredith reluctantly ended the call, but she promised to call back as soon as she could, and they all spoke their love for her and she, for them, before hanging up.

She laid her phone down and sat for a moment thinking about rivers. She had stood on the banks of the Osage River today and thought about her dad.

Her attorney had learned that Hollis Clark's body had been recovered after he'd drowned and that he'd been buried in the local cemetery. Meredith was at a loss as to why her mother had never told her this. She contacted the sexton for the location of both graves, since she was unable to remember much about her mother's funeral, and he had met with her in the cemetery earlier in the week. Even though her mother's body had been laid to rest next to her husband's, neither grave was marked, but the sexton had brought the necessary records to be able to state confidently to Meredith that these two graves belonged to her parents and placed a couple of temporary markers to reassure her.

He had commented on the lack of a headstone and when Meredith asked him how she should go about arranging for one, he referred her to a local monument company. She had gone there after leaving the cemetery and had placed an order for a double stone and had asked the proprietor to call her when it was ready so that she could return to the graveside for the installation.

Meredith abandoned thoughts of graves and headstones, then searched in her mind for something to lift her spirits and the sound of the Blake family's dear voices in her ear only moments ago gave her a soft smile, but it was fleeting.

The day of her leaving was heartbreaking for them all, especially when a devastated Carlyn ran down the dirt road after her car and Meredith had to stop and get out to kneel and reach for her embrace and promise the sobbing little child that it wouldn't be forever.

Meredith wiped away the tears that this moment now created and prayed that it wouldn't be, but she had no way of knowing. She knew that her Father did though, and she was able to find comfort in that.

Chapter Thirteen

Meredith had been so full of good intentions. She'd really tried to call the Blakes at least weekly to see how they were doing but, just as Mr. Laird had warned her, there was always some decision to be made, or some document that needed her signature, some meeting to be at, and it wasn't long before she realized that she hadn't spoken to them in several weeks.

She knew that they had probably thought about calling her, but she also knew they would have felt they might be interrupting.

Meredith did manage to get to talk to Pastor Fred when she knew Carlyn was unlikely to be around, to ask if he and Miss Marcie would allow her to send Carlyn a guitar for her birthday. She was turning ten, in about a week. Meredith longed to be able to be there, but she knew she wouldn't be able to manage it. The Wickham's house had been sold and, even though she wouldn't have to attend the closing, she did have to arrange for an estate sale that had to happen quickly in order to keep the contract's closing date from being changed, and possibly upsetting the buyers.

Pastor Fred told her that normally, he would insist that Carlyn stick to the bargain they had made, and that she would work to earn the money herself, but that their little girl never mentioned the guitar again after Meredith left, and no longer asked to be allowed to do various jobs to earn the money to buy one. He didn't want to upset Meredith, but he had to be honest and tell her that little Carlyn was grieving. This, of course, caused Meredith to grieve as well, and she was unable to keep from breaking down, during their conversation.

Pastor Fred knew that Meredith had no choice but to leave them when she did, and that it was a very difficult and trying situation she now found herself in. He told her that he and Miss Marcie had decided that they would take Carlyn to Monroe to buy a guitar on her birthday, but that if the guitar came from Meredith, it might go a long way toward helping Carlyn cope with losing her and might even "put the spark back in her eyes".

She had immediately put everything else on hold to shop around until she found just the right mini acoustic guitar, along with a very nice case, picks, capo, and a tuner, and took it to an express shipping store to be carefully packed and sent to Carlyn. She tucked in a birthday card, telling her how much she loved her and missed her, and encouraged her to keep writing her beautiful songs.

Meredith checked every day on the tracking number and was relieved when she knew the package had been delivered and signed for.

That very night, her phone rang and she answered it quickly, expecting to hear either Pastor Fred or Miss Marcie, but it was Carlyn who greeted her.

"Merry, thank you so much! It's the most beautiful guitar I've ever seen!" Her gladness and gratitude were mixed with tears, and Meredith could hear her little voice breaking.

"Oh, baby girl, you're so welcome! Happy birthday, sweetheart. " She choked back a sob. "I want you to keep working on your music, Carlyn. You're already so good, and you're just gonna keep getting better. Whenever you play your guitar, baby, just remember how much Merry loves you."

She steered the conversation to the kittens and other things that she hoped would make the child laugh and when they were ready to end the call, Carlyn promised her big sister that she would keep singing and writing.

When the call was over, Meredith laid her phone down and bent over, weeping as if her heart were crushed. She was alone now, with no one to see her but Father. When she finally got up and went to bed, she fell asleep still crying.

She knew she should probably find a church in Poplar Bluff, but the thought of walking into just any old church, where no one knew her or loved her, like the Blakes did, was something Meredith dreaded.

As she did every Sunday morning, she managed to talk herself out of going and instead, spent the morning seated at her mother's piano. She had intended to just leave it stored until she found a place that she could consider permanent, but her longing for the piano won out. Meredith had hired a moving company to transfer her mother's things from the old storage facility to one located much closer to her rental cottage in Poplar Bluff and, before they were done, she paid them extra to bring the old piano to the cottage and set it up for her.

It needed tuning badly, of course, and she was concerned that it might have come in contact with dampness or mice, but had found someone to come tune it and check it for any damage, and was relieved to hear that it had survived all those years in storage remarkably well.

Meredith sat fingering the keys now, and humming softly to a melody that she found stirring inside her as she awoke this morning. She played it with one finger, then began to lay chords alongside the simple waltz-like melody, and embellish it. By the time morning was leaning toward becoming noon, her song completed itself and she hurried to pen the lyrics and write a chord chart.

Meredith had written songs when she spent her days in "The Father's Field" and would show them to Carlyn, from time to time. Most of them had been self-healing and self-comforting. This morning's song felt different and she knew it was meant for someone else.

Look through the Eyes of Love,
See what I see.
Where there's a broken heart,
Someone needs Me.
Where there's a shattered dream,
Where there is pain,
Tell them My Story,
Tell them My Name.

And let Love heal all things
They have learned to hide.
Let it bind their wounds,
Hiding deep inside.
I know the smallest things
They are made of.
Tell them I see them
Through the Eyes of Love.

Of course, Meredith did draw healing and comfort from the song, but she knew, somehow, that Father would one day have her sing it to others who were broken and needed to be healed. She had a sense of being prepared to be sent to those people and it both frightened and excited her.

She began to wonder if Father would agree to her spending some time actually recording some of her songs, so that she could maybe leave them in the hands of people who might need to hear them.

She had looked into a few recording studios but had felt a check in her spirit, and had decided not to take the songs Father had given her to any of those places. She just didn't have a peace about it. She finally decided that she should establish a church home and maybe that would be a good starting place for her to not only get to know people in this town, but to find a way to record her music.

She gradually began visiting a few churches, although none of them felt nearly as welcoming to her as the Blake's church. Meredith forced herself to be honest, though, and admitted that no church in the world would ever be as special to her as that church. She knew she would have to lay aside all her biases and let Father lead her.

She finally returned to one of the churches she had recently visited and when several of the people who greeted her actually recognized her, remembered her name, and expressed their happiness at seeing her again, that went a long way toward causing her to consider it as a home base.

After a few months, she had attended enough to also remember names and was invited to dinner with Pastor Greg Linden and his family. During their meal, they took the opportunity to tell Meredith about some of the church's outreach programs and activities, in order to help her find a place to plug in, if she wanted to get involved.

She brightened up considerably, when she learned that the church had a coffeehouse downtown that they opened several nights a week, with live music and street ministry. She freely admitted that she was a musician and songwriter and Pastor Linden told her he'd have his team in charge of the coffeehouse get in touch with her for open mic night.

"You're doing that in faith," Meredith grinned. "For all you know, I could sing like a startled hen."

They all laughed, but Pastor Greg's wife, Tara, had an instinct about Meredith and felt the Lord was breathing on all of this.

She was right. When open mic night came around, Meredith was scheduled to sing a couple of songs. She sat down at a digital piano and began to softly play. She had a special touch on the keys that caused others to look up from their conversations and pay attention, and when she began to sing, everyone was listening intently.

She closed her eyes, as soon as she felt the anointing come over her, and sang her songs with a voice that was low, slightly husky, and intimate. Her lyrics had substance and were beautifully crafted, and her accompaniment was completely married to her vocal delivery.

The response to her music was overwhelming for Meredith, and she blinked back tears of surprise and quietly made her way back to her table. Tara Linden immediately came over and hugged her.

"My goodness, Meredith. God is going to use you in a way that can't even be imagined!"

Meredith became more and more requested at the coffeehouse and "a couple of songs" turned into half-hour sets that continued to stretch into longer ones.

The coffeehouse was such that any and all were welcome, no matter how dynamic for Jesus or how downtrodden by the devil a person was. A large portion of the people who wandered in couldn't even afford the coffee and pastries, but the church provided all of it freely.

Meredith had gotten to know a few of the homeless people and always looked for them, whenever she was onstage, silently asking Father to use her music to touch them.

She had kept her financial status quiet, even though she put untraceable cash into the offering envelopes at church and made anonymous donations to the coffeehouse. She'd located a soup kitchen that the church worked alongside and would come and sing while meals were served and leave large, mystery donations in their collection box.

Meredith had so entered into this time of ministry that her birthday came and went without any notice from her, which was a blessing. Had she stopped to consider the day, it would only have marked the single, most painful and heartbreaking day she had ever endured, but Father spared her on this first anniversary of all that, and the day innocently passed by without her even remembering.

Fred and Marcie Blake remembered, but wisely kept quiet, choosing not to call and mention a day that was now despicable to Meredith, but that had brought her into their home, their lives and their hearts.

Chapter Fourteen

Greg and Tara Linden looked up from their coffee and smiled at the late-arriving, slightly flustered Meredith.

"I'm sorry. I thought I pretty well knew where most things are in this town by now, but I ended up going to an entirely different place!"

They stood up to greet her and Tara gave her a little hug. "We're just glad you made it. We thought you might have forgotten."

A waitress spotted Meredith sitting down and came over to take her order, before she smiled at them in apology. "Well, I *can* do that, sometimes. I don't know why I'm like that, but some things, important things, can just go right out of my head, especially if I get distracted with something else."

"Squirrel!" the pastor lightly cried, with a laugh.

"Exactly," she agreed. "I try not to be flaky, but I probably come across that way."

"Not at all," he assured her. "We all have those kinds of days."

Tara seemed as if she were about to burst and Meredith looked at her with a slow grin. "Are you okay?"

She looked over at her husband and they both laughed. "We just have something we want to run by you," she replied, "but if it upsets you at all, or if you're just not interested, all you have to do is tell us, straight out, and we'll get out of your business."

Meredith wrinkled her brow and waited.

Tara deferred to her husband. "Did *you* want to?"

Greg leaned back and laughed. "Oh sure, throw *me* under the bus!" He waited for the waitress to set Meredith's black coffee in front of her and ask if anyone needed anything else, then proceeded. "This is just something that came to us, actually to Tara, and we want to run it past you, but it's just an idea and it's completely fine, if you don't want to fool with it."

Meredith simply sipped at her coffee and continued to regard them with curiosity.

"How would you feel about recording your music?"

She put her cup down and looked at the both of them in surprise. "Did I already mention something about that to you guys?"

They looked at each other and shook their heads and she smiled. "It's just that I've been praying about doing that, and I checked into some studios but I couldn't get a peace about working with any of those people, so I've been just waiting to see if Father would lead me to the right place. If I'm even meant to do it," she added.

"Oh, you are!" Tara said emphatically and her husband grinned over at her.

"Subtle."

She laughed and shrugged. "I don't care, this girl is meant to be in a studio and we both know it!"

"Speaking purely from a sense of how I feel I'm being led, I think I am, but only from that standpoint. I don't care about being known, and I certainly don't care about money, but I feel that it would be easier to reach more people if I could actually put my music into their hands. If that makes sense."

"It makes perfect sense," Pastor Greg assured her. "We know someone with a studio that we feel would be a good producer for your music. Producing, I mean, in the sense of giving you a good, clean recording and not trying to busy it up or change you in any way. He's just a kid, actually, I think somewhere around fifteen or sixteen, but he's got a great feel for music and he's especially gifted with technology. He's the grandson of one of our members. He hasn't been to church that often, but we don't nudge him. He needs to come on his own. Otherwise, he's just being pushed and that's not our way."

Tara joined in. "His name is Michael Corbett, but he goes by Mick. He records at home in his parent's basement, but I've seen it and he's got a pretty good setup. I think you'd be impressed."

"We haven't mentioned any of this to him, though," Greg added. "We thought we should talk to you first. I think he would do it for free, to be honest."

"Oh no, he wouldn't have to do that, I can pay him. I was going to pay anyone I hired, I just didn't like the vibe I got off those other guys. Money isn't the problem."

"Well... I mean, the kid would probably get excited if he found out this was a paying gig. Honestly, from what I've been told, he's pretty professional, especially for only being a teenager, without a lot of years of experience under his belt."

Meredith sat thoughtfully for a moment. "Why do you think it is, that he doesn't come to church?"

"To be honest, I think it's more about his introversion and less about peer pressure or rebellion, or anything like that," Pastor Greg replied. "Mick's basically shy, unless you're talking about music. That's the only time he shows any enthusiasm at all. But he's socially awkward."

"He's sad," Tara offered. "I mean, that's just how he seems to me. It could be that he's just stoic, but he always seems a little melancholy, to me. But he's a sweet guy and that might just be his personality. You'd like him, Meredith, whether you worked with him or not, I think."

"Here's the thing." Pastor Greg leaned forward, and spoke seriously. "Mick was at the coffeehouse the first night you sang there. I wasn't there but Tara was, and she said that something you sang really had a big effect on him. It's unusual for *anything* to have a big effect on that kid."

"I wish I could remember, now, what the song was, but I was so busy watching Mick, that I missed the lyrics," Tara admitted regretfully.

"Don't feel bad, I only sang two songs that night and I can't even remember what they were," Meredith laughed.

Tara grinned and nodded when the waitress came around to check for refills. They all pushed their cups forward and waited, before she continued.

"I don't really know what the song was doing to Mick spiritually or emotionally, but I could see the wheels turning and he was fully engaged. That's what made me start thinking about him recording your music."

Meredith felt an inclination stir inside her to at least talk with the boy and see if this might lead to something. "I guess we could give it a try," she finally said, after they gave her time to mull it over.

Tara and her husband celebrated with a high-five slap and grinned, happily.

Meredith laid her headphones down and came over to where Mick was seated at his console.

"Can we hear this on your house speakers?" she asked and he nodded.

"I always hear it different ways, to check the mix," he answered. "I like the first listen to be on the house speakers. Then I check on headphones. Sometimes, I even burn a song onto CD and check it on my car speakers."

She laughed. "Well, this isn't anything I plan on selling, so we probably don't need to go that far."

"But, at some point, you're going to mass produce these songs, right?" The normally expressionless, long-haired, awkward teenager looked over his round, wire-frame glasses at her in surprise. "You should."

"Do you think so?" She was half teasing, half humoring him.

"You should go to Nashville."

Meredith's mind immediately went back to her Christmas in Louisiana, just after Carlyn Blake had surprised her with a song she'd written for Meredith's Christmas gift. She had kidded Carlyn about meeting up together in Nashville someday, just as she had over the phone once, shortly after she'd moved back to Missouri, and Carlyn had climbed up onto her lap and confided with confidence, "I *will* live in Tennessee, someday. I already know!"

Meredith's smile was bittersweet, and she only pulled out of her thoughts when Mick repeated a question.

"Did I what?" she asked. "Sorry, I didn't hear all of that."

"Did you want to lay any more tracks, while we're at it? I mean, before I actually start mixing things."

Another song came to her mind, and she nodded. "Let's do at least one more, Mick, if you're good with that."

He responded with real enthusiasm. "I say let's keep going until you're tired of singing."

"Maybe we should order a pizza then," she laughed. "We're gonna be here a while!"

She was joking, but he brightened up, so she pulled out her phone and asked him who to call. They debated toppings and discovered that they both liked pineapple on Canadian bacon, regardless of the naysayers, and Meredith ordered their lunch, asking that their delivery driver come around to the lower level back door, so that they'd hear the bell.

Meredith relaxed and listened to playback of what they'd recorded so far, and when they were done listening, Mick repeated his earlier statement.

"You really should think about going to Nashville, Meredith."

"And do what? Hang on, there's the bell." She hopped up and met the pizza employee at the door, added a tip that made his extra trouble worth the effort, then made her way over to a table near the console, lightly tossing the large box up and down. "Hot, hot, hot!" she laughed.

Mick brought over a couple of chairs and pulled some drinks out of a mini fridge, and they sat down to do some serious damage to their lunch.

"Okay," Meredith said, after devoting a moment to just savoring that first bite of hot pizza. "Go to Nashville, and do what?"

"Top the charts, for one thing," Mick replied. "Do concerts, tour. You'd be doing all of that, if the right people heard your music."

"I don't know about that," she said, shaking her head and popping a can of soda open.

"I do." Mick looked over at her in a deadpan manner, with only the slightest bit of self-confidence. "I know music. I know when it's good and when it's bad. Your music is good."

Meredith looked at him in surprise, then shrugged. "I'm not sure all that public stuff would be for me."

"Then why are you writing and singing at all? Just for a handful of people in a coffeehouse in Poplar Bluff?"

Meredith kept mentally revisiting his question, while they replayed a couple of tracks and finished their lunch.

"I'll have to give that some thought, Mick," she finally said quietly. "I hadn't really thought about why I was doing this. It just felt like a natural thing for me to do. But I guess there must be a reason for it."

She rested her legs up on the seat of another chair and looked down at her bare feet, in an absent-minded way. "I guess I'd better ask Father about it."

Mick backed up a track, then glanced over at her. "Father? Do you folks live around here?"

She shook her head. "No, my mom has been gone for a long time, and I never did know my dad. He died in the Osage River just before I was born."

Mick nodded. "A lot of people have drowned in that river. I guess not any more than drown in other rivers, but you hear about it more around here, not being all that far from it, I guess." He stopped, and regarded her curiously. "Wait, so who's Father, then?"

"God. But He said I needed a Father, so that's what I call Him."

"He said? Like, He actually tells you stuff?" The young man seemed skeptical.

"Well, not out loud, so that you'd hear Him too, and start looking around," Meredith laughed. "It's hard to explain. It's a sort of... not exactly a vibration..." She stopped and tried again. "But it's sound, though. Sort of."

Mick looked interested. "What kind of things does He say?"

Meredith almost just shrugged and let it go, but she felt Father prompting her, as something specific came to her.

"Okay... hear me out," she grinned. "I already know how this is gonna sound, but you asked. I was lying on the couch, not too long ago and the TV was on. Probably public television, because I hate commercials, so I was just letting it drone on. Then this science show came on. I'm not a science nerd, or anything like that, but I find some of that interesting, so I started watching.

"The narrator was talking about molecules. He said something like 'scientists have long known that molecules are made up of atoms, which are comprised of these subatomic particles: protons, neutrons and electrons. However, it has been recently discovered that another particle exists. It cannot be detected by conventional means but it has perpetual movement'. And then Father said, 'That's easy.'

"So I jumped up off the couch and said, 'What is it?' and He said 'It's sound'. I felt like I was literally about to climb out of my own skin!"

Mick furrowed his brow and leaned forward. "Sound?"

Meredith nodded. "That's just what I said, 'Sound'? And Father said, 'It's the sound of My voice. It's a part of everything that exists: that couch, the chair, the trees outside, the rivers... everything that exists is held together by the sound of My voice, something that man is unable to observe, but for the fact that has movement. The sound of My voice never ceases to have movement, because it exists outside of time, with no beginning or end.' I tell you what, Mick, I think about that almost every day. There's a lot packed in there."

He watched her carefully, as if something were clicking into place for him. "So... you're saying that God talks to you and you're able to know it, even though it's not out loud because... it has movement? So, you can feel it and understand it?"

She nodded. "That's about as clearly as I can put it."

He let out a sigh. "But why would He talk to you? I mean, isn't He up there running a whole universe, or something?"

Meredith shrugged. "Because He's God. He can do whatever He wants. If He wants to talk to me, I want to listen. But He doesn't have favorites. He'll talk to you, just like He talks to me. You just have to want to hear Him and then listen."

"How do you know that it's not just your own thoughts?" the young producer challenged.

Meredith laughed and got up to head back over to her piano. "Because a lot of times, He says things that I don't want to hear!"

She sat back down to get ready to begin recording her next song and glanced up to see if Mick was ready. He wasn't. He was resting his chin in his hands, deep in thought.

Chapter Fifteen

Meredith had finally decided to just rent a boat and not commit to buying one. As relieved as she was to realize that she was enjoying her life in southern Missouri, she still somehow knew that all this was only a passing season, but that Missouri would never be her permanent home.

She hadn't taken a boat out by herself before, but she'd ridden with the Lindens on their party barge, and had even been allowed to launch and trailer it. She had since decided that she really needed to go fishing, but only if she could fish from a boat and be unapproachable, as far as someone being able to just walk up to her on the bank, and try to strike up a conversation.

She had, in fact, tried fishing from the banks of the Black River and it didn't take long for some "good ol' boys" in a pickup to stop and offer her a beer, and ask her if needed any help baiting her hook. She hadn't replied, but moved in such a way that the pistol on her hip was clearly visible and they headed off to charm someone else.

That sort of thing had been happening more and more often, lately. It seemed that no matter where Meredith went, there was always some guy trying to get to know her. Rather than feel flattered, it made her angry. She didn't mind having friends who were men; in fact, she had more male friends than female, if she were forced to count. She just had no use for men who flirted.

She had been surprised at how angry she had become when a man at the post office noticed her, and had persisted in trying to interact with her, complimenting her looks and suggesting that they go out. It immediately took her back to when her old boyfriend had adopted this same, persuasive campaign, and she could literally feel her blood pressure rising. In fact, she had been so abrupt and loudly rude to the man, that she had to sit down and talk to Father about it later that evening, but feeling remorse for her behavior did nothing to weaken her position. She had no place in her life for men, in that regard, and that was just the way it was.

Meredith's thoughts were now honed in on fishing and she was longing to go, so much so, that she visited a few boat dealerships. She had spent an entire day checking out boat after boat, firmly telling herself that she was only looking, and that buying something like a boat made absolutely no sense, as long as she was only renting the cottage, and had no plans to put down roots. A boat would just be something else she'd have to sell or tow, when the time came for her to move on. She had almost abandoned her plan to go fishing at all, and it was only when one of the boat dealers told her that they rented some of their boats, that she again became enthusiastic.

She had opted for a small, two-seater pontoon that she'd have to operate with a front-mounted trolling motor, but she didn't mind that. She just wanted room to move around, to take a lunch, and to relax. The man behind the counter recommended this small boat over more expensive boats, once he'd discovered that she'd be going out on the Black river alone.

He did advise her that it wouldn't be a good idea for her to try to pull the boat, as small and light as it was, with her little car, so she took the paper with the boat specifications the dealer had written down for her, and told him she'd been thinking of getting another vehicle anyway, and if she did, she'd be back to rent the boat.

She thought she'd be glad to trade in her old car, since it was something she'd bought used years ago, and was beginning to need more and more maintenance but, although the car had been part of a life in New Orleans that she bitterly regretted, it had also carried her safely to the Blake family and then on to Missouri, so when she let it go, it was with a bit of reluctance. She had thought about keeping it, as well as buying a new car, but she reminded herself that she could only drive one at a time.

After leaving the car lot, her first stop was at a bait and tackle shop, since she'd always used one of Pastor Fred's old cane poles that he had rigged up for her. She knew she could borrow gear, as she'd done before, but she wanted her own equipment.

An old white-haired man in overalls came around the counter to ask if he could help her and before long, Meredith had a fishing rod and a new tackle box, filled with everything she'd need for her big outing. She intuitively liked the old gentleman who owned the shop, who had a distinctive German accent, and who'd introduced himself simply as "Hoke". Meredith made up her mind that his nice little shop was on her short list of places she'd be returning to on a regular basis, especially because she could tell he had a wealth of fishing stories he could share with her.

Today, she pulled up at the boat dealership, and the man who'd helped her before came out with her to determine if the white Jeep she'd just bought would be enough to pull the pontoon. Of course, the salesman at the car lot told her it would be, but he was trying to sell a new vehicle. She wanted the boat dealer to confirm it, and he was able to.

Now, Meredith was easing the boat along, not getting too far from the shore of a river she was unfamiliar with, but keeping an eye on the depth finder, to keep from hitting any stumps or rocks. She finally maneuvered the boat into a tiny outlet of the river that veered off on its own, and got ready to fish.

Meredith smiled sadly to herself, as she pulled out bits of cut up nylon pantyhose and began putting blood bait on her hook. She remembered the way little Carlyn had wrinkled up her nose and stepped back, when she'd baited her hook at Castor Creek, and knew it had to be the same way she'd reacted herself, when Pastor Fred introduced her to this stinky way to catch catfish.

She swiped the back of her smelly hand across her cheek to stop the tears that wanted to come, and focused her attention on fishing. It wasn't until she'd landed her first catfish that she was able to break free of her deep longing for Pastor Blake, Miss Marcie and Carlyn, and begin enjoying herself.

Even grabbing the fish in Pastor Fred's recommended "lip grip" came naturally, and without yet another painful memory, and she tossed her catch into an ice chest and began to bait up for another, though she knew she'd only eat a couple of fish at the most, and was planning to throw the rest back in.

She watched other boats glide slowly by, with their occupants glancing casually over at the beautiful girl who was out on the river, all alone, but she wasn't too worried. She had her pistol with her, if it came to that, but she knew that most of the people she'd encounter today would be simple folk who just wanted to fish, like her, and who had no thoughts at all of bothering her. She finally even managed a wave to an older couple who saw that she was set up in a cove they had considered, but who now smiled at her and moved on to look for another.

Meredith had grown so comfortable in this tree-lined nook of the river, that she made sure her anchor was down, wiped her hands with some sanitized towelettes, but not without remembering Miss Marcie's trash bag of wet towels with a smile, and dug around for lunch.

She settled down cross-legged on the floor of the boat, leaning against a seat, and slowly worked on eating a sandwich, while her thoughts began to roam around.

She'd been in Missouri for almost five years, now! She stopped and double-checked her math, as that thought seemed impossible. She counted back on her fingers, using Christmases as her marker, even though she had left Louisiana in July. She was startled to realize that four Christmases had passed since that special one she'd spent in Grayson, with the Blakes.

The first one here had gone by without celebration, since she spent it alone, although the Blakes had called her and they visited over the phone. It had been too emotional for Meredith though, and after hanging up, she'd almost wished they hadn't called her. They were all she could think about, for the rest of the day.

The Christmases that followed were better enjoyed, since she spent them serving at the soup kitchen and singing while homeless people came in to get warm, be fed, and not be alone. She had spent last Christmas with the Lindens, but she had only stopped by that evening after having been at the kitchen. Still, it was good to be with people who knew her and who cared about her.

And now, another July was quickly approaching and that would officially mark five years, since she'd left the Blake's house and began to make her way alone again, in the world.

She sighed and shook her head. Sweet little Carlyn wasn't a child, anymore. She'd be turning fifteen in a couple of months! Meredith had become so overwhelmed, right after returning to St. Louis to settle her inheritance and the Wickham's estate, that she hadn't kept in touch with the Blakes as she'd meant to. Now, she was staring at five years of being parted from them and she blinked back tears, realizing that she didn't even know what Carlyn looked like, anymore. Still, she was comforted, knowing that the one thing they would always share would be their love of music and their desire to be used by God.

Meredith had more and more opportunities to sing and had begun to travel out from her church to various rallies and special services. Tara had arranged for her to sing at a regional women's conference and she was being contacted more and more, to perform concerts.

She always declined offers that asked for her testimony to be shared, however, and was firm about that. When Pastor Greg and Tara had asked why she felt so strongly about it, she simply told them that she wasn't that girl anymore, and that she only wanted to talk about what God was doing in her life now, not what she had been doing without God.

They'd both felt there was more to it than that, but neither had pushed for anything further. Meredith was clearly a private young woman and they didn't want to do or say anything that might suddenly make her uncomfortable around them. Pastor Greg and his wife had a strong feeling that, even though she was only in their lives for a season, God had chosen them to be a part of Meredith's journey and that her journey would lead her to minister to others on a much larger scale than any of them could guess.

Meredith's thoughts were slowly invaded by some showoff with a loud ski boat that charged past, creating a big wake, and rocking her pontoon so much that she had to hurry to grab her fishing rod, that was sliding toward the side.

She choked back an instinct to mutter something that was not Father-approved about the guy in the ski boat, but scowled darkly in his direction. She began to pack everything away and get ready to head back to the dock, to return the rental, and to see if she could remember how to fry fish the way Miss Marcie had taught her.

Mick Corbett hurriedly killed the track he was listening to and grabbed his phone. He'd been hoping for this call from his cousin in Nashville, who, despite only being in his twenties, was a very well-known producer with a studio on Music Row, and who was also a very influential mentor and source of encouragement for Mick. He was surprised to hear from him so soon, though. He'd sent him some music to listen to, but he just figured he'd be too busy to get around to it, anytime soon. In fact, Mick had hoped for very little, at all. He was just rolling the dice. He answered the phone with a little adrenaline rush.

"Hey, Perry."

"Mick! What's going on up in Mizzou land? Got your package, by the way."

"Oh, good deal."

"Mick... where, in the world, did you get this music? Who *is* this?"

"Oh, you mean you've already listened to it?"

"I did, while I was sitting in my car, waiting for the longest train in the world to crawl by. Desperate times," he laughed. "But maybe fate, who knows? Mick, who is this girl?"

"Her name is Meredith. She goes to my granddad's church. I've been recording her here in my studio."

"How did you land *that* gig? I'm a little jealous. Nothing this good has come through my studio in a long while, if ever, to be honest." Perry leaned back in his chair and drew in a deep breath. "What does she want to do?"

"That's just it. She's doing it, as far as she's concerned," Mick said, and the disappointment in his voice was evident.

"Well, what is 'doing it', Mick?" Perry asked. "Is she signed?"

"She not even looking to get signed."

"You have got to be kidding me!" Mick's cousin was stunned. "All this girl's got to do is walk down Music Row with this CD and she'd be snapped up in a heartbeat."

"She doesn't want that, though," Mick said glumly.

"She doesn't want a record deal?" Perry just shook his head. "Wait, then why did you send this to me? I just assumed that you knew someone who wanted to break into the industry and you thought I could help, and maybe I could, but you're saying this Meredith doesn't even want help? I'm just... wow."

"She doesn't even know I sent that to you," Mick confessed.

"Okay, so go back to where I interrupted you. You said she's already 'doing it'. So, what is it she's doing?"

Mick flopped back in his chair and shrugged, even though Perry couldn't see him. "She's doing some local concerts in the church's coffeehouse, and maybe some rallies and conferences but she's mainly hanging out at a soup kitchen, either serving meals or singing while the homeless eat."

"And all that's awesome," Perry said, "but why is she letting you record her, if she doesn't plan to do anything with the recordings?"

"She *is* doing something with them. She's giving them away."

Perry sat speechless for so long that Mick wondered if their call had dropped out.

"I'm here, I'm just trying to... " Perry Mitchell blew out a loud breath and stared hard at nothing. "Is her mind made up, Mick?"

"I don't know and that's one reason I sent the music to you. I feel like she's meant to be in Nashville, but she just shrugs and grins, every time I talk about. It's pretty frustrating."

"I can see why!"

They both sat in silence for a few seconds, neither sure where to go with all this.

Finally, Mick spoke up. "I feel like if I could just talk her into going down there, just for a few days to get a feel for the place, it might start her thinking about aiming a little higher than local rallies and coffeehouses. I wonder..."

Perry waited for him to continue, and he finally did. "I wonder if she could meet with that guy you know. The one who has the big label and the management firm."

"Joel Etheridge?" Perry asked.

"That's the guy."

"Well, it'd be great, except that Joel has pretty much put the kibosh on anyone trying to send him new talent. The last time he was in here, he was more than a little steamed about a local promoter trying to do an end run around him, to get his artist in the front door. That didn't set well. He's definitely developed a 'don't call me, and I won't call you' attitude."

Again, they were both silent for a while, each lost in his own thoughts.

"You know, Mick," Perry began quietly. "I'm not trying to do an end run, myself, but Joel's associate might be the one to hear this girl's music. If anyone has a chance in a million of getting Joel to at least listen, it would be Marshall Edwards, but even then, Joel doesn't ease up for anyone, even if they're friends, so Marshall might just strike out, himself. Still, though, it might be worth a shot."

Mick stared absently at his console. "The trick would be getting Meredith to even go to Nashville, at all. If I tick her off, she may just tell me to take a powder."

Perry laughed. "Is she a bit of a hothead, then?"

"I'd have said no, if you'd asked me a few months ago, but something's going on with her. She's either changing, or she's getting relaxed enough to let her real personality come out, but either way, she's no pushover. I'm not sure what's going on, there."

"How old is she, Mick?"

"Well, older than me, for sure. Maybe even ten years older. But she doesn't look like it. She looks like someone I could be going to school with."

"Not that it matters to me, but Nashville is Nashville," Perry said dryly. "Does her face match up at all with her talent?"

"She looks like a model," Mick returned simply, and Perry raised his brows.

"And she just wants to serve soup and sing at a coffeehouse?" He sighed. "Well, Mick... all I can say is good luck to you, convincing her to come here. But if you ever do, call me, and I'll try to set up a meeting with her to at least find out if there's any chance at all of getting her to consider doing more with her music. That girl could be selling out concerts in no time, but you know that, or you wouldn't have contacted me."

"I know," Mick conceded. "She's supposed to come back later this week to listen to my mix on a couple of tracks. Maybe I'll try again. Thanks, Perry, for calling me back."

"Thanks for sending those songs. Let's not give up just yet, Mick. She just might surprise us."

Chapter Sixteen

Meredith fixed her expressive eyes on Mick and listened, so still and quiet that it made him a little nervous. He didn't know if she was going to seriously consider what he was saying, or if she was about to yell at him and leave.

He finished and just sat there, toying with his headphones and waiting.

Meredith very well *might* have yelled at Mick, were it not for the fact that she had been awake all night, talking with Father about the direction she seemed to be headed with her life. She knew she was meant to relocate, hopefully toward somewhere permanent, and had asked Him if she could just go back to Louisiana, but that wasn't in His plan, she could tell. It disappointed her, but she wanted to be obedient.

She sat now, with her arms crossed, looking down at the floor, but saying nothing.

"I'm sorry, Meredith," Mick offered tentatively. "I know I should have asked you first. I don't really have an excuse, except that I know you're meant to do more than just sing locally around here and I wanted my cousin, Perry, to hear your music. I knew he'd be honest with me."

"And your cousin is in Nashville?" she asked quietly.

Mick nodded. "He has a studio on Music Row. He's pretty involved in the Christian music industry, and in big demand as a producer, so I knew he'd be the one to ask."

"The Christian music *industry*, huh?" Meredith grinned.

Mick smiled at her, tremendously relieved that she didn't seem to be upset with him. He had come to think of Meredith as a friend and he'd hate to know that he'd ruined that. He had so few real friends in his life.

"So it's a big machine, then, I guess," she said flatly.

"I mean, yeah, even Perry says it is, but he's not onboard with all the hype and jockeying for position that he says goes on. He's more focused on what a person is called to do, than what they're good at doing, and if they're not called to use music as a means of ministry, then they're just wasting his time and everyone else's."

Meredith widened her eyes in astonishment. That was a pretty in-depth statement to come from the normally reserved Mick Corbett, and her look of surprise even stirred a little laugh from him.

"Those are all his words, I'm just a parrot."

She smiled and resumed studying the floor, while her thoughts seemed to keep returning to something Father had said to her last night. *"I've called you to swim against the current."*

She raised her head and viewed Mick quizzingly. "What do you know about salmon?"

He seemed thrown off by her strange, out-of-the-blue question. "So you want to change the subject, then," he said, clearly disappointed.

"No. I want to know what you know about salmon."

He surveyed her closely, trying to determine if she was serious, or just kidding around. "I know they swim upstream."

She nodded. "That's about all I know, too. But that's what Father said, last night."

"Salmon?" Mick looked even more lost than ever. At least the whole 'molecules' thing made sense, but salmon?

"He said 'I've called you to swim against the current'. I've only heard of salmon doing that," Meredith mused, thoughtfully.

"Salmon aren't the only fish to do that. Other fish do, as well," Mick shrugged. "Some trout do. Catfish do. Well, channel cats, anyway."

Meredith raised her brows and hoisted herself up so that she could sit cross-legged in her chair. "Catfish? Are you sure?"

"One of those things they told us in school. Why would they lie?"

She mulled that over. "But if I go to Nashville, how is that swimming against the current? Won't I be just another girl singer? Aren't we a dime a dozen?" She scowled at some mental image that this question conjured up.

Mick gave her a steady look. "You won't be just another girl singer for a lot of reasons, Meredith. Besides, if God puts you with specific people, it's because He chose them to help you swim upstream. Just like here. But there." He grinned when she laughed at him.

"Well... I'll think about it, Mick, and I'll talk to Father about it. If He's good with it, He'll show me and if He's not, He'll let me know that too, believe me. He has no problem saying no to me."

"Okay, but make sure you keep your own thoughts out of this," Mick pleaded, despite his intention to not push Meredith too hard and have her not go, just out of spite. "I mean..."

He raked his hands through his long hair and let out a sound of frustration. "That didn't come out right. I meant that I want you to try not to already have an opinion, when you talk to God. Dang it!" He looked completely put out with himself and Meredith laughed and reached over to give him a little punch on the arm.

"Stop. I know what you mean." She was fine with what he'd said. "I'll make sure, I promise. I don't wanna mess this up."

Meredith had no idea where her cell phone was. She had left her hotel room to go back down and search through her Jeep, but it was nowhere to be found.

She came back up to her room now, and stood looking around, just trying to guess where she could have mislaid it.

"Marco!" she said with a grin, then belted out a loud laugh, when her phone said "Polo" by ringing.

"That is just *too* funny!" She reached underneath the suitcase that she'd just tossed onto the bed, and pulled out her phone and answered.

"You were supposed to let us know you got there okay!" Tara fussed.

"I was going to, but I couldn't find my phone, so you beat me to it. I'm glad you called, though, that's how I found it."

Tara smiled and shooed Bagel, their gentle, lazy Beagle, off the chair before claiming it for herself. "So, how do you like Nashville, so far?"

"I have no idea. I've seen the freeway, the exit for my hotel, and now my room. That's about it." Meredith wanted so badly to be barefoot, but she wasn't sure about hotel carpets, so she sat scowling at her shoes.

"Do you at least have a view?" Tara asked.

"I guess," Meredith replied, with a characteristic shrug. "Buildings. So there's that."

Tara laughed and absently rubbed Bagel's head, when he gazed up at her as if she were talking to him. "You never sound like it, Meredith, but you have to be excited!"

"I do?" Meredith lifted one brow. "Is that a rule?"

Her friend laughed again. "Yes! I think it's the law in Nashville. You have to be excited!"

Meredith lifted her long curtain of dark hair and twisted it into a thick rope before letting it rest over one shoulder. "I'm all agog, then," she grinned.

"Seriously, Meredith, I know this is God! You know how sometimes you can just tell?" She assumed Meredith nodded and plodded on.   "I can just tell.   This is God!"

"I'm glad one of us can tell," Meredith returned, with a stifled yawn. It had only been about a four hour drive, but she was feeling it, for some reason. Probably because she'd been up all night, she decided.

Tara heard the yawn and laughed. "Okay, I can take a hint. Grab a shower if you want to wake up, or lie down if you want to go to sleep, but don't stay in the middle."

"Words to live by," Meredith grinned.   "This is me, lying down."

She'd only been lightly napping but she still had trouble orienting herself when her phone rang again. She groped around until her hand located it and answered without opening her eyes.

"Yes. I'm still excited," she said blandly to her overly enthusiastic friend, Tara.

"Well, that's our first hurdle cleared, then," a male voice declared, with a little laugh.

Meredith opened her eyes and sat straight up. Who, in the world, was this guy and how did he get her number? "Sorry, I didn't look to see who was calling. I thought you were a friend of mine."

"Well, I sort of am, by proxy," the caller assured her, "if Mick is still your friend."

Meredith relaxed, but only a little. "Mick is, but that doesn't automatically qualify *you*."

He laughed and she allowed herself a brief smile. "I'm Mick's cousin, Perry. He didn't tell you that he'd given me your number?"

"He did, but I just got here. I certainly didn't expect a call right off the bat. Besides," she shifted around to get comfortable, "I thought I was meant to come camp outside your Music Row studio with a cardboard sign that says 'will become a superstar for food' and stare up at you with puppy dog eyes."

"No, don't do the puppy dog eyes. I won't be able to take you seriously." Perry laughed again. "Everyone tries that on me. I'm immune."

Meredith grinned and settled back against her pillows. "Well... let's hear it."

"Hear what?"

She shrugged. "You called *me*, remember?"

He toyed with a pen and grinned, only able to imagine the face behind this personality.

"Well, I saw your cardboard sign and I guess I just need to know what you want to eat."

Meredith actually laughed and he felt a bit of relief. She wasn't completely inaccessible, then.

"Catfish," she responded lightly.

"I don't have any on me, but my folks have a cabin by a lake, and they swear it's full of catfish."

Meredith widened her eyes, as things just got a lot more interesting. "Keep talking."

Perry decided to risk it. "Seriously, Meredith, you drove all this way. I'm sure it wasn't just to buy boots. Can I talk you into at least coming by the studio and volleying a conversation back and forth? I just want to hear your thoughts about what it is you feel you're being prepared to do."

Meredith was quiet for a moment. That had been the right thing to say to her, but she wasn't sure if it was genuine or manipulative.

Perry waited and she finally responded. "Can I pray about it tonight and call you in the morning?"

He let out a silent breath, a little deflated, but remaining hopeful. "Sure. My number came up on your screen, right? It should have."

She checked. "Six-one-five is you, I guess. So, yep."

"Call me on that number, instead of dialing the studio directly, if you don't mind. I'm between receptionists right now, and most calls go to the machine and I just sort through them later."

"Is that proper Music Row etiquette?" she joked, with slight sarcasm.

"Nah, but Music Row can get over itself. Let me know either way?"

"I will."

She ended the call and got up to stroll over to the windows and pull back the drapes. She studied the busy Nashville streets, the tall buildings and the forest of neon signs, with a frown.

What was she doing here? Had Father really nudged her to do this?

"Nothing I'm seeing out this window appeals to me at all, Father," she said sadly. "Can I really not just go back to Grayson?"

"We've spoken of this," He reminded her gently.

"I know." She hung her head and began to feel tears gathering. "I sure miss You, though. I miss our field."

"I came with you," He assured her. "I told you that I would never leave you."

"I know, but..." She wiped her cheek impatiently. "It was our place. I'm sorry, I'm just a little lonely."

"Am I not enough?" He questioned, regarding her with compassion.

"You're more than enough," Meredith replied, with a smile. "I don't know what I'm feeling right now."

"It's time to leap again, and you're worried you won't land safely." He smiled down at His child. "But I'll catch you."

Meredith stood silent for a long moment before she pulled the drapes closed, and came over to reach into her suitcase for the satchel holding her mother's Bible.

"I want to show You something," she whispered, forgetting that He already knew. She turned through the pages until she found the portion of Genesis she was looking for, and held it up for Him to see.

"You told Abraham to just take off and leave everything, and go somewhere vague and... well, basically, You pretty much just said 'I'll let you know when you get there'. And he just up and did it!"

"Abram," Father corrected. "His name had not yet changed, not until I confirmed My promise and established his new identity."

"You didn't tell him anything at all about where he was going." Meredith said glumly. "That's what this feels like."

Her mind traveled back in time and she heard Miss Marcie's voice so clearly, that she laid her hand on her heart, to protect it. *"Honey, it's my belief that if you get in your car and take off again, you ain't got any idea where in the world to go to."*

"She was worried about you," Father cut in, knowing her thoughts, "because she knew I wasn't sending you. You would have been running away, again. It may feel the same to you, but when I send you, it's not the same, at all."

"Are you sending me, Father?" She looked up anxiously, with tears that insisted on running hotly down her beautiful face.

"I Am," He replied. "But you are not alone. I was with Abram. I Am with you."

"Will I get a new name?"

"Someday, yes."

Father's peace came around her like an embrace, and her countenance began to reflect the willingness to trust, that was stirring inside her.

"I love you, child," Father breathed.

"I love You back."

Chapter Seventeen

One of the hardest things Perry Mitchell ever had to do was to show no reaction, whatsoever, when looking up from his console and discovering one of the most beautiful women he'd ever seen. Nashville was crawling with women who'd come there counting on their looks to land them the prize they were after, and Perry had, for the most part, become immune, as he had jokingly told Meredith, on the phone. But he'd never seen anyone yet who was as much a natural beauty as Meredith Clark.

Fortunately for him, Mick had warned him, not only when he'd told Perry that she looked like a model, but again this morning, when Perry had called to let him know that Meredith had agreed to come by the studio today.

"I should probably warn you about her eyes," Mick had stated, in his toneless, detached manner.

Perry had been taken aback. "What about her eyes, Mick? What's wrong with them?"

"They're gray."

"That's it? Okay..." Perry had laughed.

"No, but I mean... they're... she has beautiful eyes, but don't tell her that. Seriously."

Perry was clearly puzzled. "Don't tell her? Is she sensitive about her eyes?"

"In a way," his cousin said. "Not necessarily about her eyes, I don't mean that. But she's just sensitive, period, if any guy says anything to her about her looks. She doesn't like it. She might even just get up and walk out."

Perry drew his brow, clearly confused. "I don't know that I've ever met a woman who didn't like to hear compliments."

"You're about to," Mick said flatly. "Don't do it, Perry, or you'll blow it."

"Does she hate guys, or something?" Perry persisted.

"Not all guys. I mean, she and I are good friends. I think it's guys who are potentially available that she has no use for."

"Am I supposed to invent a wife, or something? I can't just run out and rent one, because Meredith Clark doesn't want to work with single guys." Perry leaned back and laughed, but Mick wasn't amused.

"Perry, she has a story. I don't know what it is, and I doubt you'll ever know, because Meredith is private. But whatever her story is, I can tell there's a man in it, and it didn't end well. She gets way too angry for that not to be true.

"I rode with her to pick up some hoagies on one of our session breaks, and this man walked over and handed her his business card and told her she had a pretty smile. That's all he said, and she went off on him. She seriously ripped that guy up one side and down the other, and it took her most of the afternoon to pull out of it, and be able to focus again. I mean, it was just simple flirting, as far as the guy goes, but something about it triggered her and she made him sorry he'd ever said anything.

"I'm begging you. No matter how much you might be tempted, just keep things platonic because if you don't, she'll just hop in her car and take off."

Perry knew that all this was hard for his cousin to say, and that made him more willing to listen.

"Well, I certainly don't plan on upsetting her, Mick, but I'll remember what you said and try to be careful."

Perry had hung up the phone and mentally replayed the conversation he'd just had with his cousin and was now so resolved to not upset Meredith Clark that, when she came walking into the back door of the live room, as he'd told her to do, he was ready to greet her. He saw her come in and look around and drew in his breath sharply. "You weren't lying, Mick," he muttered, before coming out onto the live room floor to welcome her.

"Meredith?" He simply reached out a hand to shake hers and kept his tone casual. "Nice to finally meet you."

She regarded him warily, but smiled and very briefly accepted his handshake.

"Find this place okay?" he tossed out lightly, gesturing toward the seating area just beyond the control room. She held back and waited for him to lead the way.

"It wasn't all that hard, once I mastered the whole traffic circle thing," she replied. "Whoever dreamed that up apparently had too much time on his hands."

Perry laughed and motioned toward some chairs. "Sit anywhere you like," he invited. "Well, I say all sorts of disparaging things about the traffic circle everyday, but no one listens. I guess it's here to stay."

He offered her something to drink and she responded with, "I never turn down black coffee". Perry was glad, because he felt he needed some sort of prop in his hands, to be able to settle down and talk with this woman, and a cup of coffee would be just about right.

"I just made this," he said, coming back from the coffee pot with two cups. "I hope I didn't get it too strong."

"No such thing." Meredith took the cup and settled back into her chair, eyeing him curiously over it, as she raised it for a sip.

"So... " She looked around appraisingly. "Did you get Mick started in recording, or is that some sort of gene pool thing?"

"I might have, but it wasn't by design," Perry admitted. "He came here for a couple of weeks a few summers ago, and he just sort of hung out here, since there wasn't much else for him to do, when I was working. So I let him shadow me and it didn't take long for me to realize that kid has natural talent. I'm a little bit proud of him," he grinned.

"I like working with him," Meredith said. "He gets me."

"Well, if you end up doing any recording here, I may have to send for Mick, to make sure that I dial in on whatever his formula is," Perry laughed.

"Oh, don't worry," Meredith returned, giving him a pointed look. "If it's not a flow, I'll tell you. You won't have to guess."

"Actually, it's that sort of thing I'm interested to hear," Perry said sincerely, relaxing back into his seat. "I'm sure you must have had a similar chat with Mick, at some point, and it sounds like he listened. But more importantly, Meredith, I'm most interested in hearing what you think God wants you to do with your music, even more than I am to hear about your technical and stylistic preferences.

"Those are important," he hurried to add, "but I get a sense, after talking with Mick, that there's a ministry component to your music that goes beyond being known or selling records, or even touring. But all of that really contributes to your reaching more people, on a larger scale. That's all part of the big picture, so I'd like to step back and get a better sense of what you're painting."

"An art critic," Meredith murmured, smiling and looking away at nothing.

"No, not a critic," Perry assured her. "I couldn't possibly criticize what God is doing with you. I just want to understand it, so that you and I can decide if there's anything I can do to help you get to where you're going."

By now, Meredith had managed to kick her shoes off, after Perry's carpet passed inspection, and was now sitting with one foot tucked under, and the other resting on the floor.

"Don't get me wrong, Perry," she said, inspecting a cuticle before glancing up at him, after a moment. "I'm actually more appreciative than I let on, but I can't help wondering what's in it for you? I don't exactly have a good experience, as far as men who want to help me. Well," she added, remembering Pastor Fred with a soft smile, "for the most part."

"One day, when Perry Mitchell was innocently minding his own business," he began, with a grin, "his phone rang and who should it be, but Perry's cousin, Mick?"

"I know all that," she grimaced with a little eye-roll. "But what made you willing to get involved?"

"Mick," he insisted, more seriously, this time. "He wouldn't waste my time. Mick is maybe even more critical than I am, when it comes to singers, so when he sent me your music and then appealed to me on the phone for any help I could offer, I had no choice. Besides, I heard your music myself, remember? I may not be as hard to please as Mick is, but I do have *some* standards."

"So you don't just produce anyone who walks in here, throwing money at you?" Meredith asked, with enough of a smile to take the edge off her question.

"I do not," he replied, simply. "I turn away more people than I schedule, even if they're already signed to a label. Most record executives in this town know that I don't curry favor and I don't get involved with projects I don't feel a connection with. Well..." he paused, to correct himself. "There is one label here in town that I consistently work with, whether I personally like the artist I'm sent, or not, but only because I respect the owner, and I normally end up agreeing with him, at some point."

Meredith pulled her other foot up into the chair and crossed her arms, with only the faintest of smiles. "Are you sure he's not some sort of Svengali?"

Perry laughed at that. "You'd have to meet him, to understand. Actually, it's my hope that you will, someday, but it's almost easier to meet the Pope, around here. He's... not a 'people person' and he's a bit short on charm."

"But he's in the music industry?" She widened her beautiful eyes. "I thought all you Nashville cats did, was sit around charming each other all day, and admiring each other's heavy, pointy awards."

Meredith made Perry Mitchell laugh without even trying. She was a good conversationalist and he rarely got to just sit and bat a good chat back and forth, like this.

"Joel Etheridge is not a mixer," he stated, and Meredith was aware of the smallest bit of current that gently surged through her, when he said this.

"Should I know that name?" she asked, drawing her brows, with a genuine look of bewilderment on her face. "I can't remember ever hearing it, but it sounds like a name I should know."

"You'll know it pretty quickly, if you're here for any length of time," Perry informed her. "But if you don't keep up with the industry, or watch any sort of award things, then I wouldn't expect you to know the name. Maybe it just sounds like something else familiar to you?"

"Maybe," Meredith agreed, although she had a sudden flashback of what Father had told her about molecules. This felt like that.

"Well, Meredith, how attached to Missouri are you?" Perry hadn't meant to switch topics so abruptly, but he had been wondering if she had plans to move to Music City.

"I'm not attached at all, I'm just originally from there. I was away for a while, but I ended up going back there to... move some things into storage," she finished quickly. "I can live anywhere, I guess."

"If it turns out that you like the area and want to rent first, I have a friend who's a developer and he has some new condos and apartments just being finished on West End. They're pretty nice, and some of them, I think, are even pet friendly, if that's a thing."

"It's not," she said. "I happen to like animals, so I wouldn't do that to one."

She said this with a straight face, but he laughed, anyway.

"I'm gonna jot down his name and number," Perry said, reaching into his pocket for his card and, at the same time, remembering what Mick had told him about the guy at the hoagie shop. "He might already have something that's move in ready."

He scrawled a few things down before holding the card out to her and she took it, but very slowly and not without looking at it carefully in his hand, first.

"Thanks," she said simply.

"Can we move to the console room and fire up what Mick sent me?" Perry asked. "I'd like to hear it again with your input."

"Guess so," Meredith said with a sigh. "Since I already have a pair of boots."

This time, Mick was the one finding a CD in the mail.

He'd listened to it in his car, driving back from the post office, and was listening again, in his studio. As soon as he finished, he called Perry's number and left a message for him to call, then went back to just soaking it all in. He closed his eyes and began to focus on all the intricacies and nuances of the music and became so engrossed, that his phone rang several times before he realized it.

"Mick!" Perry had almost given up on him and was getting ready to play phone tag. "I guess I don't have to ask what you're doing," he grinned.

"No, you don't," Mick admitted.

"Well, I was gonna email it, but I remembered how much fun you have sitting out in that old Vega of yours, listening to music, so I went old school, and saved you the trouble of having to burn it, yourself."

"My Vega is a classic and I paid a lot of money to have that player installed in it," Mick laughed.

"Well, I believe you got your money's worth, today."

"I did. I opened the package at the post office and played it on the way back here. I'm listening to it on the house speakers, now. It's awesome, Perry," Mick said, sincerely. "I mean, it's really special."

"Well... that means a lot, Mick," his cousin replied. "Thanks, buddy."

"The only down side to all this is that Meredith isn't around anymore, but it's for the best," Mick said, with a tinge of regret. "I miss having her around, because I can't see ever having another musician of her caliber in here again, but she was just wasted, here."

"Well, with all due respect to Poplar Bluff, I have to agree," Perry replied.

"Where did she end up?" Mick wondered. "One of those condos?"

"For now, an apartment. She's out on West End though, and if I'm being honest, I think she hates it because of all the traffic and noise, but I expect she'll stick it out for a while. She says she hates moving and apparently, she's done a lot of it."

"She has. When I met her, she had just moved here from St. Louis, I guess, and there was something about New Orleans, but when she mentioned that, she was suddenly done sharing. She did say she was ready for something permanent, but I knew it couldn't be here. Not with a voice like that."

He started to say something else, stopped himself, then decided to go for it. "Perry... what's the vibe between you two? I mean, she's a beautiful girl, but..."

"Not to worry, Cousin," Perry quickly reassured him, with a grin. "Meredith is living proof that a man can't build a lasting relationship with someone strictly based on physical attraction. She can get on my last nerve, and I guess I tick her off every few minutes, as well. We are so much alike, that we've become like 'buds', or maybe even siblings. The more time we spend together, the less I'm aware of her beautiful face and the more I'm aware of her irritating quirks. And she's got 'em in spades!"

He laughed and Mick breathed out a sigh of relief. "Good, because that means she'll stay put, and you'll probably end up being her only producer. She's not the kind of girl who's going to let some label guy steamroll her and pair her up with someone she doesn't like."

Mick leaned back in his chair and propped his feet up. "Speaking of that, what happens next, Perry? Any chance of you getting her into that Etheridge guy's office?"

"Right now, I'd say no, Mick, but I'm not through trying. My hope was to get her to meet Marshall Edwards and that might have just fallen into my lap, on its own."

Mick raised his brows and kept listening.

"She asked me if I could recommend a good church and, of course, I told her about Covenant Fellowship. It's where I go. Gary Brenner would be a good fit for her, as far as a spiritual covering. And that's honestly why I was quick to tell her about it, but, fortunately for me, not only does Marshall and his wife attend that church, but Etheridge does, as well. In fact, I think a lot of his staff go there."

Mick grinned and stuck a fist up in the air with a silent "yes".

"I'm hoping that God will breathe on that whole thing and that no one will be able to accuse me later of manipulation but, honestly, Mick, I would, if I had to."

"I hope so!" Mick said this with more animation than Perry had ever heard from him, and he couldn't help laughing.

"Come down, sometimes, Mick and crash at my place. She'd love to see you again, and you could hang with us at the studio."

Mick's face lit up. "Road trip!"

$\mathcal{P}astor$ Gary Brenner smiled down at the beautiful girl Perry had just introduced him to, and took one of her hands into both of his, in a fatherly clasp. His white hair reminded Meredith a little of Pastor Fred, and when she smiled back at him, it was genuine and heartfelt.

"Welcome to Tennessee," he said, his eyes crinkling with humor. "I hope you come back to see us."

"She just moved here," Perry volunteered. "She's doing some recording at the studio."

Pastor Gary raised his brow in delight. "Listen, Meredith, if you want to use us to practice on, you just let me know. Not just here, but we have a coffeehouse ministry."

Her amazing eyes lit up. "Do you know of any kind of soup kitchen or something like that, I could sing at?"

This time, it was Gary Brenner's eyes that lit up. So many of the musicians who flocked to his church seemed to be on the lookout for talent scouts, and had no time for that sort of thing, but here was this girl, who could easily grace the cover of any fashion magazine, asking to be allowed to sing her songs in a very humble and obscure setting. He laid his hand on her arm.

"Meredith..."

"Merry, if you like," she offered. It was the first time she'd invited anyone to call her that since she'd told Pastor

Fred and Carlyn that they could, the day they found her on the side of the road. "Like Christmas, I guess. It's spelled that way."

"Merry." He continued to beam down at her with true interest, not seeming to realize that other people were hoping to speak with him, after the service. "There's a homeless shelter right in downtown Nashville. Is that what you were meaning?"

"That's perfect," she said, grinning up at him, unable to hide her enthusiasm.

"Well, I'll call the powers that be, and see if we can set something up," he said, giving her shoulder a little pat. "Perry can let me know how to reach you."

Meredith flashed him a happy grin and thanked him, before letting Perry gently steer her over to another couple she had noticed, but thought they were waiting to talk to the pastor.

"Meredith, this is Marshall Edwards and his wife, Bobbie," Perry said. "This is Meredith Clark. She's new to Tennessee and she's currently in the studio, doing some spec work."

Marshall gave Meredith a friendly smile and a little handshake, but raised his brows in surprise. Perry Mitchell never let anyone do spec work in his studio! What was this about?

Bobbie leaned in and gave Meredith a warm hug. "Hey there, sweet girl," she said in such a loving way that Meredith came very close to becoming teary-eyed. The last woman who had hugged her and spoken to her with such affection had been Miss Marcie.

"Hi," she said very quietly and gave Bobbie a soft smile.

"What kind of work are you doing in the studio, Meredith?" Marshall asked. "Pitching lyrics, or..."

Meredith looked over at Perry, who spoke up. "To be honest, Marshall, I'm helping Meredith put enough tracks together to build a project."

Marshall was clearly stunned. He'd be tempted to think that Perry was simply smitten with this beautiful young woman, if he didn't know Perry better than that. Perry was a complete professional and it wouldn't matter to him how breathtaking a woman was, if she wasn't talented. For Perry to let Meredith do spec work could only mean that he held her in high regard, as a musician.

"Are you recording original material, Meredith, or covers?"

"My own stuff. Building a catalog, I guess, and if we have enough strong tracks, maybe plan a project."

"You're not signed, then?" Marshall questioned, looking from Meredith back to Perry, who shook his head.

"But she will be, when it's time. That's all it is, just a matter of time."

Marshall was intrigued. Perry Mitchell had never been this adamant about any artist.

"Will you be singing anywhere around here, Meredith? Bobbie and I would love to hear you."

"Oh, I hope so!" Bobbie exclaimed.

"Well, I asked the pastor if I could sing at the homeless shelter and he said he could arrange it," she replied, missing the wide-eyed look Marshall and his wife exchanged. "And he said something about a coffeehouse. I was doing that in Missouri."

"Pastor Gary's gonna call me to set that up," Perry let them know. "I'll be in touch."

"Do that, Perry. Call me anyway, tomorrow, if you get a chance. I have a few questions."

Marshall and Bobbie let Meredith know how glad they were to have met her and took their leave, and Perry watched them go with a look of peace resting on his face.

"And so it begins," he murmured to himself.

Bobbie Edwards dabbed at her face with a tissue that was really too damp now to do any good. She was so caught up in the lyrics of Meredith's song that she felt as if she were the only one in the room.

Meredith sat at the piano on the coffeehouse stage with a single overhead light bathing her long, beautiful, dark hair with a golden sheen. Her eyes were closed, as she traveled down the path of her song, one that Father had given her recently, as she was working her way through that uncertain part of her journey she called "that Abraham thing".

> *The graves are dug, but oh, so hard to fill.*
> *It hurts to die, and rise to do Your will.*
> *Like vapor dreams, life's never what it seems.*
> *I do remember,*
> *I asked to learn surrender.*
>
> *I walk with You, not knowing where we're going.*
> *Stops are few, but peace comes from knowing*
> *Though aching, I'm better for the breaking.*
> *So tender,*
> *The heart that's learned surrender.*

Meredith's voice was beautifully low with an unaffected rasp and huskiness that drew the listener in. She sang with an intimacy that Marshall Edwards had never heard.

She played the piano with a mastery that hinted of classical training, although Perry had told Marshall that she played by ear, and this song was embellished by minor chord progressions that were unexpected and haunting.

Build an altar, pitch a tent.
Learn the rules of your covenant.
Give it all, then give the rest,
And still, He gives the best.

How far to go? Will I survive?
How will I know when I arrive?
The final prize
Is never found in compromise.
The mighty contender
Will find it in surrender.

Meredith let the piano journey on past her lyrics and quietly rest in a minor chord that remained unresolved.

The immediate response from the audience was deafening. Meredith simply gave them all a slight nod and the hint of a smile, then quietly returned to her table, but not before being asked for an autograph by one bold teenager. Once others saw that she didn't seem to mind, they asked for the same favor.

Meredith simply signed her name, and the date and location, and if someone seemed to want to talk to her about how God was speaking to them through her music, she gave that person her full attention, especially to one girl, who knelt down by Meredith's chair and looked up at her with pleading in her eyes.

Meredith lowered herself down beside the girl and just sat on the floor with her, bending her head down to hear what she was saying, while music was being played in the background, and then whispering her responses. She had her arm around the young girl and after a while, the girl's face changed and she broke into smiles and wrapped her arms around Meredith's neck. Meredith closed her eyes and hugged her back and then said a couple of other things quietly to her, before they both stood and the girl left with a light in her eyes.

Meredith watched her go, before she turned around to realize that she had just left Perry, Marshall and Bobbie waiting. She was also startled to discover that Pastor Gary had come in and was sitting at the table.

"I'm sorry," she began, but Bobbie stopped her.

"Don't you ever say that again," she admonished her, still overcome by the ministry that had just taken place. "God has first priority. The rest of us can wait."

Pastor Gary stood up and came around to give Meredith's shoulder a little squeeze. "This needs to happen a lot more often, Merry."

She raised one hand and patted the one that rested on her shoulder. "I don't have much else going on," she grinned. "Just let me know, I guess."

"I will certainly do that!" Gary Brenner assured her, looking around the table at the others with a happy smile. "There are all sorts of places God would like to use His children, but so many times, it's not flashy enough or important enough, in their eyes, and so they keeping waiting for a better offer. But I can promise you, Merry, that as long as you have such a willing heart, there is no shortage of ministry opportunities ahead for you. You just hold on to your hat!"

❧❦❧

Marshall Edwards sat looking at Perry over his coffee cup, and just shook his head.

"I just wish there was some way, Perry," he said, not even bothering to hide his frustration. "But Joel has said an emphatic and impatient no to everything that's come across his desk for months, now. He's back in Oklahoma this week, dealing with something for his mother, some legal matter, but I expect when he rolls back into town, he'll be as obstinate as he was, when he rolled out."

Perry nodded and sat musing over Marshall's words, not really sure where to go from there.

"I know it's not fair to ask, Perry, and I apologize for even doing it, but please don't shop her to another label. Not just yet, anyway." Marshall raked a hand through his hair and let out a breath of disappointment. "Of course, I realize it's not right to just put Meredith on hold, like that."

Perry let out a breath and rested his eyes on his friend. "That's the only good news I can give you, Marshall," he said. "Meredith couldn't care less about being signed to a label."

Marshall looked up in disbelief and Perry couldn't help smiling.

"It's true. If it were up to her, she'd just sing at the homeless shelter and the coffeehouse and be content."

"We can't let her just park right there, Perry," Marshall said insistently. "Those are great ministry outreaches, and God bless her for being willing, but she can't just camp out there, like that. More people need to hear her music than just a handful of people in downtown Nashville."

"You'll get no argument from me," Perry assured him. "I had hoped that Joel would have been at church when she came and met all of you, but of course, he was out of town. It just figures. Because I know, if I could have introduced them, he would have wanted to know about her. Not because she looks the way she does," he hurried to add. "We both know that beautiful women practically throw themselves at Joel Etheridge and he pays no attention to any of them. But, with Meredith, there's a quality there that draws you in. I can't explain it, because I can't even identify it, but it's there."

"I can," Marshall said, simply. "She's anointed."

Perry sat and thought about that. "I believe you're right, Marshall."

"It's so obvious," Marshall insisted. "That girl is nothing like those silly people who come into the office and wax on and on about how music is who they are, and it's the most important thing in their lives, and how they would just 'die' if they didn't have their music. No wonder Joel has just about had it, with this town!"

Marshall nodded for more coffee before finishing. "Meredith isn't a musician who ministers. She's a minister who uses music as her pulpit. She's obviously anointed to do it and even born to do it, unlike so many who make that extraordinary claim. You can tell this girl spends time with God and the ministry that comes out of her is the overflow of that."

"That's just what I had hoped you would see, Marshall," Perry said quietly. "It's just too bad that Joel Etheridge can't be the one to see it."

"Well, don't give up just yet," Marshall said, with a grim determination washing across his face. "In the meantime, I can provide some local concert opportunities for Meredith, have her do some openings, and perform during set breaks."

"Marshall, that would be awesome!" Perry's smile lit up his face. "If we could proceed as if Meredith *did* have a contract, maybe it would lead to one. Sooner or later, Joel Etheridge has got to notice her."

$\mathcal{Bobbie}$ Edwards stood next to the outdoor stage, not trying to eavesdrop, but unable to pull herself away.

Meredith had just stepped down after her performance, and she had been stopped by a girl who was crying and pouring her heart out. Meredith was staring at her with a look of pain on her face that Bobbie could almost feel.

Marshall Edwards approached his wife, and joined her in observing the quiet, but emotional interaction.

"What's going on, Bobbie?"

"It's another young girl, wanting to talk to Meredith, but this feels different," she said, in a low voice. "Look at Meredith."

Marshall couldn't miss the tears beginning to run down her cheeks or the look of absolute anguish. He wondered if this was something he should interrupt, but Bobbie laid a hand on his arm.

"If she didn't want to talk to the girl, she wouldn't, Marshall. There's something else going on, here."

By now, the young girl was smiling up at Meredith, but Meredith's own smile was shaky and uncertain. The girl gave her a hug and rejoined her friends, leaving Meredith wrapping her arms around herself, in an attempt to feel some sort of protection.

Bobbie immediately went to her and gathered her up into a secure embrace. "Come on, baby, with Marshall and me," she insisted. "They're about to wrap things up here, anyway."

Meredith was still shaken and let them lead her out to their car. She had ridden to the concert with them, and was relieved that they were ready to take her back to her apartment.

She slipped into the back seat and Marshall began to drive toward West End. It was only when Bobbie heard a real sob coming from Meredith, that she had Marshall pull over to let her open the back door of the car, and sit down beside her. She put an arm around Meredith and just let her lean on her shoulder and cry, while Marshall continued heading toward her apartment.

When they arrived, Meredith didn't make a move to get out of the car. Instead, she sat, with her eyes closed, clutching the tissues Bobbie had pressed into her hand, and trying to both apologize and explain.

"Honey, you don't have to tell us anything you don't want us to know," Bobbie soothed, lifting a wet tendril of hair from Meredith's cheek.

She took a deep breath and after a long quiet moment, said, in a dull, listless voice, "I do, though. You should really know everything, I guess, in case you don't want to help me with the music, anymore."

"If this is something about your past, honey, that's between you and Jesus," Marshall said, in a kind, firm voice and she gave him a sad, little smile.

"I did hear some of what that girl said to you, Merry," Bobbie confessed. "I heard her mention her suicide attempt."

Meredith nodded and looked down at the wad of tissue that was beginning to fall apart. "She said some of her friends took her to one of my concerts after that, and while she was there, she prayed to be saved."

"That's wonderful, Merry," Marshall said, looking into his mirror at her tear-streaked face.

"Yes," she agreed, with a little wet sigh. "It is."

"But, honey, that wouldn't have upset you," Bobbie observed gently.

"No, it wasn't that," Meredith agreed, accepting the fresh tissues Bobbie gave her when she saw more tears beginning to form.

Meredith folded her arms, but lifted one hand to rest her forehead on. "So you heard the whole thing about her trying to commit suicide?" she asked in a whisper.

"Just the fact that she tried, nothing else." Bobbie said. "I'm so sorry, sweetie, to have overhead."

"No, I don't... it doesn't matter," Meredith said, softly. "But the reason she tried to kill herself..." She let out a little moan and began crying again and Bobbie quickly tightened her embrace and began comforting her.

"We don't need to hear the rest of it, baby, if you'd rather not tell us. You don't have to," she said, continuing to move Meredith's long hair out of the path her tears were making.

"I guess I need someone in Tennessee to know," she finally murmured. "I just feel so alone, right now."

"Meredith, anything you need to tell us will never leave this car," Marshall assured her quietly.

"Thank you," she said, wiping at her cheeks and taking a deep breath.

Slowly, and with much difficulty, Meredith told Marshall and Bobbie Edwards what she'd had to admit to Miss Marcie, about why she'd fled from New Orleans.

After she had worked through the agonizing ordeal of having to put the events of that horrible day into words, Marshall and Bobbie walked her to her door. They both gave her hugs that underscored their love and commitment to her, and assured her that not only had she been forgiven of all that, but that someday, God was going to make something beautiful come out of those ashes.

Those sweet words were to come back to Meredith, many years later, from a much loved, but unexpected source, and it would heal her in ways she couldn't imagine.

Meredith had stopped her Jeep so unexpectedly, that the vehicle behind her had to swerve into the next lane to keep from plowing into her. The driver had given her a sharp blast of his horn, but it was completely wasted on a beautiful, starry-eyed, young woman, who hadn't even heard it.

She had parked against the curb and jumped out of her Jeep and was now standing in front of tall, beautiful gates that were closed, but that invited her to look beyond at the treasure they guarded: a beautiful, massive, gray-blue Colonial Revival home, in the distance, at the end of a driveway that ended in a large circle. The setting was like something out of a magazine and Meredith raised a hand to her throat as she realized that the sign just outside the gates really was a realtor's sign and not some sort of advertising.

Meredith never had much use for her cell phone and would, more often than not, either lose it or leave it, but she dashed back to her Jeep now, and was rewarded to find it on the floorboard, where it had slid when she hit the brakes.

She hurriedly dialed the first number on the sign, and was surprised that the realtor, who identified herself as Kendra Massey, answered the call so quickly.

"I was wondering, please, if the house on Old Hickory Boulevard is still available?" She hurriedly added the street number and took a deep breath.

If the realtor had said no, Meredith was convinced she would have thrown her phone down onto the ground, gotten back into her Jeep, and had a good cry. Instead, the realtor assured her that not only was the home still available, but that she had placed the sign there herself, only a couple of hours before.

"Please, may I see it?" she asked breathlessly, and Kendra Massey noted the sense of urgency in her voice.

"Absolutely! Are you free sometime, today?"

"I am," Meredith assured her. "I'm in front of the home now, but I can come back, if you need me to."

Kendra promptly decided that a successful sale took priority over a brown sack lunch at her desk, any day of the week, and reached for her keys. "I can head over there now, if you're good to wait. I'm about ten minutes out."

"Oh, I can wait," Meredith assured her, her heart beginning to pound with excitement. "Thank you!"

Meredith was still standing at the gates, with her face reflecting the anticipation she was feeling, when Kendra pulled up behind her Jeep and got out, walking toward her with some papers in her hands and a smile of greeting.

"Isn't it beautiful?" she asked, holding out her hand to shake Meredith's. They exchanged names before Kendra lifted the cover on the gate's keypad and entered the code. She pressed another button to hold the gates open and give Meredith time to drive her Jeep through, then allowed them to close behind her own car, before following her around the circle drive and stopping in front of the stately home.

Meredith got out of her Jeep without even realizing it. She stood gazing at the large, deep porch, the intricate moldings and the wide, welcoming front door, with its leaded glass detail. She had no way of knowing that the look of happiness on her face made her even more beautiful. Kendra crossed her arms and watched her taking it all in, before she spoke.

"Would you like to see the grounds first, or go inside?"

"Oh..." Meredith couldn't choose. "I guess, I'll defer to you. Just show it to me the way you'd want to see it."

Kendra raised her brows and gestured to the right. "It's beautiful, inside and out, but since it's such a gorgeous day, why don't we take a look at the grounds, then?"

She led the way around to the side of the house. The same black, steel security fence that separated the property from the road and housed the double gates was replicated in a shorter version here, with a small single gate that gave access to the sides and back of the property.

Kendra let Meredith walk ahead of her and stood back to watch her reaction. Meredith raised a hand to her cheek and let her eyes roam around, silently registering the beauty of this lovely sanctuary. Massive magnolia trees, along with pines and other evergreens spiced the air with scent and graceful willows and ornamental grasses invited her to come see their lovely pond.

"Now, this may be a deal breaker," Kendra laughed, "but this property is almost seventeen acres. It's very unusual to find something this large in this part of Nashville, but the property was in the same family for generations and when the last of the family put it on the market, they had no interest in splitting it up."

"Oh, I'm so glad!" Meredith exclaimed, joyfully.

"I am too, then," Kendra laughed. "Some people hear 'acres' and they immediately express a reluctance to have to mow grass."

"I haven't done a lot of mowing, but I feel pretty sure that I'd enjoy it."

"Maybe the first few times," Kendra joked. "Presently, there's a landscaping service on retainer. I suppose they could be kept, if you like them. Their current contract is with the sellers, so whoever buys this property would either need to hire them or make other arrangements.

They were standing by the pond but Kendra now pointed off to a small grove of trees and Meredith drew in her breath. A cabin! She looked at Kendra with wide, happy eyes, and Kendra laughed. She was enjoying showing this property more than any other she could remember. It was so much fun to see it through Meredith's eyes.

By the time they'd seen most of the grounds and had come back around to the front entrance, Meredith was all in. She hadn't declared that, yet, to her realtor, but she didn't even need to see the inside to know that this was her forever home, at least while she was on this earth.

Happily, the inside was as beautiful as Meredith could have dared to hope for.

The living room had floor to ceiling windows and the wide stone fireplace gave the room a comforting feel. She moved along silently, as Kendra took her through the double glass doors into the dining room, then on around to the kitchen and the pantry and utility room.

"Now, there is a downstairs bed and bath, just beyond the dining room." Kendra had almost forgotten that, but doubled back now, to show her. Like the living room, it featured floor to ceiling windows and had a beautiful view of a stand of magnolias, stone benches and a small fountain.

Meredith couldn't stop smiling. She followed Kendra up the wide, shallow staircase and the realtor paused before opening one of the doors at the head of the stairs.

"There are four bedrooms on down the hall," she informed her, waving her hand in the direction they would soon be moving. "One is the master, with its own bathroom suite and nice big closets, and the other three have access to two large bathrooms, and they are really something! We'll get to those, but I want to show you this room first. Now, Meredith, this room, you'll either love or hate," she warned. "It's not a bedroom, it's more of a studio, I guess. Maybe one of the family members was an artist, I don't know. The floors are rustic, and I can't tell that they've ever been restored since they were installed and the windows... well, let's just say, I hope you like windows."

Kendra opened the door and let Meredith step in first. The room seemed to have been waiting for her and exploded into radiance, not just from every window, but from a huge skylight. Everything was golden, and Meredith immediately had a vision of her mother's piano finally finding its home.

She folded her hands together like a prayer and lifted them to her mouth and her eyes were so filled with tears, she could barely focus.

"Kendra," she whispered, in a voice layered with one beautiful emotion, after another, "Where do I sign?"

Chapter Twenty

Perry Mitchell closed his eyes, crossed his arms, leaned his head back, and eased the swing on Meredith's front porch to and fro slowly, with one foot.

"Hey, Perry, I thought..."

"Shhh!" He flicked a backward hand toward her, without opening his eyes. "I'm listening to the birds. Go away."

Meredith giggled and kicked his foot to one side. "Get up! You said you'd help me, and this is where I find you."

Perry opened his eyes and leveled them at her with annoyance. "We've got all day. Anyway, we can't do much until the movers get here."

"There's a ton of stuff to do, are you kidding me?" Meredith crossed her own arms and gave him a scowl.

"I don't smell any pizza. You said there'd be pizza," he grumbled.

"I'm not gonna *make* it," she said, staring at him as if he'd lost his mind. "Who do I look like, Julia Child?"

"So no pizza, then."

"It's called delivery," Meredith said. "But they don't just show up. You have to call and invite them. Pineapple on mine," she reminded him.

"Weirdo." Perry pulled out his phone and looked for the closest place. "Pizza for how many?"

Meredith twisted her lips and did a mental head count. "Just five, I think. You, me, Marshall, Bobbie and Preach."

"Preach!" Perry grinned down at his phone, still looking for the number. "How does Gary like being called what he does?"

She shrugged. "I didn't ask him."

"I'm glad you don't call me Produce," he said, waiting for someone to pick up.

"In your case, it'd be *pro*-duce," Meredith corrected.

He laughed and held up one finger as his call was answered, and ordered three pizzas, one of them Canadian bacon with pineapple. "Yeah, we've got a real nut-job over here," he explained to the guy taking his order, and laughed at his response.

Meredith flopped down onto her first purchase for her new house, a vintage, white, metal glider, and gave Perry a petulant look.

"Oh, stop it," he grinned. "I left a lot of aspiring recording artists and superstars in the lurch today, by coming over here to help out Grouchy Gerta."

"You're the one who's grouchy," she returned. "I bet I messed up your hot date. You could have brought her along, you know. Who is it this week? Wait, let me guess... Lilah Cummings, for sure."

Perry shook with silent laughter, as he ensconced himself, once again, into the cushions on the porch swing. "Oh, hardly!"

"Pay-ree, dahlin'," Meredith said, in a sugary sweet accent, "Why, you-ah just a stinkah for leavin' yore lit'l ol' Lilah high 'n dry, when you promised me dinnah! You bad boy-ee!"

"Stop!" Perry laid a hand on his stomach, which was hurting from laughing. "She's not that bad!"

"She's worse!" Meredith insisted. "Why, I do decla-ah, Pay-ree, you jus' run off to help that ol' Murradith 'thout so much as a by yore leave, and broke my hahrt!" Meredith grinned, as her friend wiped his eyes. "And who's she kidding, anyway, by calling herself Lilah, I like to know?" she demanded. "Like we don't all know her mama named her Delilah, so own it!"

Perry threw one of the pillows at her, with good aim, hitting her in the face. "Goof," he pronounced.

"I thought I was Grouchy," she reminded.

"You're so gifted, you can handle both."

"We can still invite Lilah, you know," Meredith said with a sly grin. "I'm sure whatever she has going on, she'll ditch it for a chance to date the great Perry Mitchell."

"I thought about dating *you*, when I first met you, but only for about an hour and half," he commented with a fake air of condescension.

"Why an hour and a half?" She wrinkled her brow.

"That's when the shyness wore off and you wouldn't shut up. It didn't matter *what* you looked like, we were so over!"

Meredith belted out a laugh and he grinned at her, before standing up to investigate the sound of a large truck out on the boulevard and reporting over his shoulder that the movers had arrived. He was more than a little surprised at the size of the moving van.

"How much stuff did you have at your apartment, girl?" he said, looking over at her with raised brows.

"It's not from the apartment, I rented that furnished. This is from Missouri."

"They must have left out at daybreak," he commented, mostly to himself. "Well, they made it, that's the important thing. It's gonna take them another minute, though. They'll have to block a few lanes of traffic to get that thing backed in here."

"Wait, what? It's circle drive!" Meredith exclaimed. "Why would you back an eighteen-wheeler all the way up here, when there's a circle drive..."

She saw the "gotcha" look on Perry's face and gave him a deadpan expression that only added to his overall amusement.

He stepped out onto the stoop and watched the big truck lumber toward the house and noted, with a grin, that Marshall and Bobbie had somehow managed to pull in right behind it.

"Perfect timing." He turned around and said this to Meredith, nodding toward their car.

She stepped down to greet them and to be ready to show the movers what would generally go where.

"I can't believe you're making those guys take a piano all the way up the stairs."

"They get paid to do stuff like that," she argued. "Anyway, I'll tip them."

"When everybody leaves, I want you to take me down to the basement and show me where you print all your money," Perry said, giving her arm a little jab.

She just shrugged and smiled to herself.

The movers had put all of Lydia Clark's furniture in general areas around the house, and the old piano was resting in its permanent home, adding another beautiful element to what Meredith was already calling her music room. The big truck had departed back to Missouri, and Meredith had already given several mini tours.

The music room had created the biggest impression. It was dazzling today, and the blue skies and bright sun seeming to be actually trying to come inside.

Bobbie had been all over the house several times, just staring and enjoying every nook of it.

"I can't believe you bought the Emmons estate," she said, repeating herself, and shaking her head. "I have actually stopped outside the gates before and just looked at it. Of course, some of the family were still living here, then. It wasn't for sale. To be honest, I never thought this place would ever go on the market. I just figured they'd keep it in the family."

Meredith was curious about all that, but at the same time, glad to know that the beautiful house was all hers. Perry had kidded her that it was really the bank's and they were just lending it to her, and she let him think that with no response, other than her characteristic shrug.

"We're really gonna have to launch this girl's career now, Marshall," he said, reaching for a slice of pizza. "She's needs to start raking it in, to pay for this place."

Marshall laughed and agreed, and Meredith just grinned and headed off to answer the door.

"Hey, Preach!" She stepped back and let Gary Brenner in and closed the door behind him.

"Hello there, Merry! Congratulations!" He handed her a beautiful flower arrangement and she stared up at him in real surprise.

"Wow... these are amazing. Thank you so much!" She instinctively gave him a hug and he laughed and said, "Just adding a pop of color. Flowers are about the extent of my decorating skills, but they seem to go with any decor."

He stopped and looked around the beautiful room and just shook his head. "The Emmons place, my goodness! Will you be giving tours?"

"The next one is in twenty minutes," she informed him and he laughed.

He heard the others and started to head into the kitchen, but Meredith stopped him. "Perry seems to think you might not like me calling you Preach. I'm sorry. I didn't mean anything by it, it just slipped out, that first time."

"Are you kidding? I love having a nick name!" He patted her on the cheek. "Don't listen to Perry, he's just jealous!"

She smiled and brought him into the kitchen, along with her flowers. "You'd better hurry and get some pizza, Preach, before Perry scarfs it all down."

Gary pulled up a chair and took the slice out of Perry's hand, which filled the room with laughter. Meredith stood looking at the cozy, happy scene with gladness in her beautiful eyes, and with a full heart.

Meredith squinted and looked closely at something that seemed to be moving toward her. She was sitting out in the morning sun on the back patio and at first, thought she'd imagined it, but it was definitely some kind of animal, and it was coming from the back of the property toward the house, not running, but moseying, as if out for a stroll.

She kept her eyes trained on it and a smile washed over her face when she realized that it was a cat, and not just any cat. It was a large, gray, longhaired, beautiful cat, who finally arrived and stopped to look up at her with pretty green eyes, as if waiting for her to invite him in.

"No trespassing," she laughed, reaching down a tentative finger to see if he was friendly. He was more than friendly, apparently. He shoved his head against her hand and began purring loudly.

"You're a big ol' baby," Meredith crooned and gathered him onto her lap. He was remarkably light to be so big, and Meredith decided that he was mostly fur.

She checked him for a tag or collar, but found nothing. Her inspection did turn up one surprising discovery, though. He was declawed!

Meredith frowned. "Who, in the world, would let you outside, with no way to protect yourself?" She certainly hoped that he had just wandered off, on his own. She hated to think that someone would have just thrown him out, like that.

She got up, cradling the big cat in her arms, and brought him inside, putting him in the utility room, while she figured out how to set him up with a temporary litter box and to see what she possibly had to feed him.

He stood patiently and waited, seeming to know that she was working for him, now. Meredith found a leftover pizza box and lined it with foil. She brought in some dirt from one of the flower beds and her face wore a nostalgic smile, as she remembered Pastor Fred and Miss Marcie rigging up a litter box on their screened porch for four very lucky newborn kittens.

She put the box inside the utility room and had Big Gray Cat stay there, while she rummaged through the fridge to see if there was anything inside that was still good. Meredith had a bad habit of letting things spoil in her fridge, but the chicken breast was from last night, so she knew that was good.

She took it out and shredded it, only zapping it in the microwave long enough to take the chill off, and brought that, a plastic bowl and a bottle of water back with her.

Big Gray Cat was looking at her with adoring eyes, now. She laughed at his expressive face and put the chicken down and poured the water into the bowl and set it nearby.

"Okay, I'm gonna leave you for a little bit, so don't tear up my utility room, trying to get out," she admonished. "I'm gonna make a little store dash to get you some things, until I can find out who you belong to."

He paid her no mind, since there were other, more pressing things that needed his attention.

She made a quick trip down to a nearby store and picked up litter, a scoop, a new box, dry cat food, canned cat food, spring water, a plush bed and a few toys. She knew it was overkill, but she didn't care. She liked the idea of someone to share her very big house with, even if someone was a cat.

When she came back, the cat was napping over in the corner of the utility room on a pile of laundry. Meredith roused him with her toe and let him know that Santa had come early.

It was obvious to Meredith that this cat had clearly once been an inside cat, for more reasons than having been declawed. He knew exactly what a litter box was for and he had immediately adapted to his surroundings.

In the days and weeks that followed, Meredith made every conscientious effort to find the cat's owner, putting up flyers, going online, even placing an ad in the Nashville paper. She wondered if he had belonged to the ones who had put the house on the market and just slipped out and got left. She asked Kendra Massey to find out. Kendra called back and told her that there'd been no pets.

She secretly hoped no one would respond and, after enough time had passed and she felt she had exerted a reasonable amount of effort, she claimed him as her own and the big fluffy boy seemed to be more than willing to take up residence.

It was when he was up in the music room with her one afternoon and she was trying to write a song, that she gave him his name. It seemed that every time Meredith came around to the part of the song that repeated, the cat would quietly meow. She began to pay attention and he only did it at that one particular place in the song.

She scooped him up into her arms and brought him over to the piano, using his paw to play a few soft notes.

"We wrote a song, Hookline!" She giggled at his placid look of satisfaction. "But I pay you in vittles and luxury accommodations, so don't expect any royalties."

Hookline eventually became simply "Hook" and was Meredith's constant shadow, confidant, and buddy.

Chapter Twenty-One

Meredith's favorite place in the house was, of course, her music room, but a close second had to be her window seat, downstairs.

She spent hours nestled in it with comfortable pillows, Hook, and best of all, Father. Autumn was silently and vividly coming to Tennessee and the grounds of her property were alive with color. She would sometimes go outside to walk around in it, but more often, she would enjoy it from the many views her music room offered or, today, from the cozy comfort of her window seat.

It was hard for her to believe that she'd been living in her beautiful home for well over a year, closer to two! In fact, two of her hated birthdays had passed while living here, but the house seemed to know how to shelter her from all that and she'd simply let that dismal day pass by, just wandering the property, or hanging out in the sweet little cabin that was near the pond. She'd thought she'd use the cabin for writing, but the music room won out, so it was left to be only another hidden gem of the estate that she sometimes checked on, but not often.

She'd retained the groundskeeper that the previous owners had always used, so the acreage was consistently beautiful and inviting, but Meredith had been going outside less frequently than she did at first.

Something about being outdoors with the trees and flowers made her long for the Blake family. Sometimes, Meredith would go long periods without thinking of them, but when they did come to mind, the pain of being without them was still keenly felt, even after all these years, so she'd begun mainly staying indoors.

Because her house was so quiet, Meredith spent a lot of time talking with Father, even though Hook thought she was talking to him. He usually responded by looking at her with his eyes half closed and offering an occasional purr, although, beginning to grow fat and lazy, he usually just fell asleep.

Today, though, Meredith was writing in her journal. She'd had a dream the night before that both disturbed her and comforted her, and had certainly intrigued her.

She was back in "The Father's Field", as she always thought of it, after her little Carlyn wrote a song with that title, just for her.

She was sitting in the tall grasses that were gently waving about in the gentlest of breezes. The sun was kissing her face and the friendly cardinal had stopped by to tell her she was "pretty, pretty, pretty".

The dream was so vivid that Meredith could smell the Bermuda grass and alfalfa and could hear the singing branch, calling for her to learn its melody and hum along.

As she had done so often in days gone by, Meredith sat with her eyes closed, just experiencing the scents and sounds and listening to the music of the field. She heard steady movement in the grasses, that sounded as if someone were walking through them and smiled to herself, thinking that Father was coming to once again visit with her in their special place.

She became slowly aware that something was blocking the sun from her face. She opened her eyes but, instead of

Father, a man appeared before her. He stood straight and tall, and had curly hair that was tousled about by the light wind. The sun behind him kept her from seeing his face but she could tell that he was smiling down at her and she wasn't afraid.

When he spoke, his voice was deep and rich, and somehow comforting, and he simply said, "Father told me I'd find you here." He reached out his hand to her. Meredith took it and was lifted up to stand close to him, almost seeing his face, when she woke up with a start and a little gasp, sitting straight up with her hand on her heart, and staring around her room, in wonder.

Marshall Edwards sat nursing his morning cup of coffee and glanced up with a smile for his wife, as she plodded into the kitchen with a yawn and a comical "yes, I'm sleep-walking, so just deal with it" expression.

He waited until she'd sat down with her own coffee and had a few sips before even speaking. She'd let him know when the coast was clear.

She could tell he had something on his mind and gave him a single thumbs-up and a grin, before returning to her coffee drinking.

"Wakey, wakey," he teased.

"I'm up. Why aren't you at the office?" she suddenly wondered, looking around for a clock.

"I'll leave in a bit. I don't have anything before nine."

"What's going on in that head of yours?" his wife demanded. "I can hear the wheels turning, from here."

"Joel," he replied, almost despondently.

Bobbie nodded, but made no comment.

"I came down from my office yesterday to stop by and ask Delores when I could sit down with him and before she could even answer me, I could hear him through his door, reading someone the riot act."

His wife raised her brows in surprise. "Who was he talking to?"

"I didn't ask Dee, but it was clearly someone who'd been a little too pushy about landing his artist a deal with Joel's label."

Bobbie just shook her head and sipped her coffee in silence. It was her opinion that Joel Etheridge's secretary, Delores, heard all kinds of versions of the riot act being loudly read through that door, on a regular basis, if she were forced to admit it.

"I just told her I'd check back another time." Marshall let out a cleansing breath and leaned back in his chair, giving her a sober look. "Bobbie, if I can't get Merry signed pretty soon, some other label is going to swoop in and snatch her up."

"What makes you think she'd even agree to that?" she asked, studying him closely. "I mean, she'd have a little say in something like that."

"She's been in Tennessee for almost four years, Bobbie, and even though she likes to joke that she's only here to buy boots, she's here because she's called into the music ministry. How long can she be expected to just hurry up and wait?"

"Hold on!" Bobbie sat up straight. "Go back. There's no way she's been here that long!"

"Do the math," her husband said, with a bit of exasperation. "She was in that apartment for over two years, and she's been in her house almost as long, or at least it's getting close. She's had four Christmases in Tennessee.

Gary told me that, and said she's spent every one of them at the homeless shelter."

"I know. She turns us down every year, for both Christmas and Thanksgiving. I plan to keep asking her, but I already know I'll get turned down every time, even though she's always very grateful and sweet about it. But, I still can't believe she's been here that long."

His wife held up her hand, to buy enough time to do her own math. "That's just crazy," she breathed, and Marshall nodded.

Bobbie shook her head. "We all go to the same church. I mean, I know it's a big congregation, but you'd think Joel would have met her, by now."

"Joel's been out of town on weekends more than he's been here, and whenever he *has* been to church, he's slipped in late or slipped out early. It's like he can't sit still. I expect he doesn't always go to first service, anyway, not when he has two more to choose from.

"Plus, he always feels like people are lying in wait for him, to pounce on him with their demos, so I can't blame him. I'm surprised he even comes at all, to be honest. Anyway," Marshall added, "if I introduced them at church, it would just be Joel thinking I was trying to set him up with another beautiful woman, and he'd resent that, and might even be rude to her. I wouldn't want that."

"I hate to tell Mr. Etheridge, but I wouldn't be so quick to be rude to Meredith Clark," Bobbie laughed. "He just might wind up having the riot act read to him!"

Marshall had to laugh with her. "On one hand, I know that if Joel got behind Meredith's career, it would take off like a shooting star, but on the other, they'd probably end up fighting like cats and dogs. Meredith doesn't have the proper amount of awe and respect to put up with any of Joel's stubbornness. She'd hand it right back to him!"

They both sat with silent smiles, considering all that, before Marshall spoke again.

"Bobbie, Perry says he's gotten a couple of calls from labels wanting him to put them in touch with her."

"Oh, great!" she groaned. "And the first thing they'd do is try to turn her into some spandex-wearing, overly made up clone of every other girl singer in this town."

Her husband nodded, then raised his eyes to hers. "I can't let that happen."

⸎⸎⸎

Hook felt he'd contributed enough to Meredith's songwriting for the moment, and after allowing himself to glance toward the window, in a bored fashion, at a squirrel in a nearby tree, he launched himself off the piano bench to check out a patch of warm sunlight on the rug.

She smiled down at him and returned to her lyrics, a look of concentration shadowing her face with a slight frown. Maybe she was just feeling a little depressed, she decided.

She'd tried talking to Father about it, but sometimes, rather than answer her straight out, He'd remind her to open her Bible and hear from Him that way, which was a little harder for her. She'd been so sure that Father had led her to Tennessee and, in spite of Perry Mitchell's jokes about buying boots, she had been certain that her music was why she was here. Lately, she hadn't been so sure, but what else could she do?

She had never done anything else beside sing, to make a living... that, and a little modeling. The unwanted memory of all that was hastily slapped away, and a scowl darkened her pretty eyes, deepening her frown.

She lifted her lyrics from the piano and silently read through them.

196

What kind of fool would hit the ground
Like some fatalistic seed
Of what was once a call?
You've laid your sacrifices down
And waited for a fire
That did not always fall.

When you let yourself,
You still look back
And cry for what you've lost.
Did you really think
There wouldn't be a cost?

She admitted to herself that she would probably never sing this song in concert, but it still needed to be written.

You've crossed the sands of many years,
Through a dry and wasted land
On your way to who knows where.
Your hands are filled with souvenirs.
There are pictures of your pain
And tokens of despair.
Tell me, are you sorry
For the miles that you have trod
On your journey to be called
A friend of God?

She sang the chorus to herself in a faint whisper.

Your seed of faith has fallen
To the ground and died.
Nothing that you did could save it,
No matter how you tried.

One day, the ground will open.
One day, it will break free
And you will see it...
A strong and mighty tree.
A strong and mighty tree.

That chorus should have encouraged her, but instead, it only intensified the longing inside her to move forward in what she believe God had led her here to do.

It's sometimes altars, sometimes graves.
Are you called to be an Isaac,
Or is Lazarus your name?
It's sometimes mountains, sometimes caves,
Where the darkness is not threatened
By your feeble flame.
Still, your song will echo
From beyond your prison walls,
And your Friend will hear and answer
When you call.

She repeated the previous chorus, before closing her eyes and just sitting with her head bowed. She could feel Father sitting with her, and smiled down at her hands.

"Hello," she offered, with a little sigh.

"Hello," He returned.

"It's that Abraham thing again, isn't it, Father?"

He gave her a gentle embrace, knowing what she meant.

"It's that Abraham thing."

Chapter Twenty-Two

Marshall Edwards flashed a grin at Joel Etheridge's secretary, Delores McGee, and paused by her desk before heading into his office.

"How's the weather, Dee?"

She laughed at their routine method of determining what Joel Etheridge's current state of mind was. "Cloudy with a chance of afternoon thunderstorms, so don't say I didn't warn you."

He raised his brows, and rested on the corner of her desk. "Does he have anybody scheduled that could end up cutting this short?"

She shook her head. "In fact, he told me to clear his schedule out this afternoon, and spread it all over into the rest of the week."

"Is he feeling okay?" Marshall was genuinely concerned, since he and Joel were good friends and, if he was under the weather, it might be wise to just postpone today's meeting.

"I think he's just aggravated and overworked, and he needs to take some time off, to be honest, Marshall," she replied. "But, of course, no one can suggest anything like that to him. He'd just have to prove them wrong, so I say nothing and do what I'm told."

He nodded, completely understanding. That was the official position of most of the employees at Etheridge and

Associates. It was best to not back Joel Etheridge into a corner and, even though Marshall Edwards was the "associate" the firm's name referenced, he was no exception to Joel's tendency to snap, when he found a situation to be particularly grating.

"Well, I should probably have my head examined, Dee, but I guess I'll risk it. Pray for me."

They both laughed and she buzzed Joel's office and was told to send Marshall in.

Joel Etheridge was staring down intently at a stack of papers and merely gestured for Marshall to come have a seat. "How's it going, Marshall?" he asked, without looking up, and not actually waiting to be told.

"All good," Marshall returned.

Joel said nothing but simply flipped a page back and then over, his brows drawing and a frown resting on his face, as he was unable to find whatever he was looking for.

"I can come back," Marshall offered quietly, and Joel glanced back up at him with a look of surprise.

"Why would you do that?"

"Well, you seem pretty busy," Marshall pointed out.

Joel closed his folder and leaned back in his chair, reaching his hands up and behind his head, to rest it against his laced fingers. "If you wait to come back when I'm not busy, I'll probably never see you again."

"I have no comeback for that," Marshall laughed. "I know the truth, when I hear it."

Joel grinned, unaware that when he did, he was an entirely different person, and nodded toward the large envelope in Marshall's hands.

"You come bearing gifts, I see. I hope you kept the receipt."

Marshall drew in his breath. This was not exactly going to be a walk in the park.

"All I ask, Joel, is that you listen to me. I'm just asking you to respect me enough to not just tune me out."

Joel narrowed his eyes and studied his friend closely. "Do I make you feel that I don't respect you, Marshall?"

"I can't really make that accusation, but then again, I've been laying low the past few weeks, trying not to get hit by friendly fire."

Marshall smiled when he said this, but Joel didn't. He continued to regard Marshall with a quiet analysis that would have been unnerving for anyone else who didn't know him as well as Marshall did.

Joel finally breathed out a sigh of fatigue, and raked a hand through his mass of unruly curls, that were beginning to be touched with gray, despite his only being in his late thirties.

"Dee told me you had dropped by when I was on the phone, apparently yelling at Kevin Harris."

"Oh, is that who you were talking to?" Marshall chuckled. "Everyone yells at Kevin Harris, why shouldn't you?"

"Exactly." Joel's grin returned, but with more sarcasm than before. "The guy's like a drunk woodpecker."

Marshall's laugh was spontaneous and Delores heard it through the door and laughed, herself.

Joel smiled at his friend, and then leaned forward to rest his forearms on his desk and look at him with clear, blue eyes that were full of questions but also goodwill.

"I wouldn't have brought you on as an associate, Marshall, if you were just someone else on the payroll that I'd rather not have to deal with personally. You're where you are because I do respect you, so let's get that out of the way."

"Well, I appreciate that, Joel. I just hope you still feel that way in a few minutes."

Joel leaned back and studied him. "Is something in that envelope liable to upset me?"

"If you're consistent." Marshall took a deep breath and decided to just swing for the fences. "Joel, are you done signing any new talent at all, period?"

"That would be an odd policy to adapt, for a record label, wouldn't it, Marshall?" he asked quietly.

"Normally, I'd say yes, but we're not talking about just any label. You've been sending everyone who approaches you away with a firm, and sometimes loud no, so I guess I'm not feeling too optimistic."

Joel turned his chair just enough to look out toward the huge wall of windows that framed the Nashville high-rises and rooftops. He crossed his arms and seemed to be reflecting on something for a moment.

"I'm just sick of the same old auto-tuned, conveyor belt music, the same wild-haired boy bands, who are too cool for school, and all the scary, rag-wearing, female 'sirens for Jesus', Marshall. All the weird vocals that are disturbingly unnatural and affected and, let's face it, just clones of other unnatural vocals, not to mention the trendy new 'watch me worship' gimmick. And then, there are the songs that wouldn't die, because the singer falls in love with his or her own voice, and won't stop singing, hyping up the crowd, and trying to pass that off as the anointing. I'm just about done with all of it."

He turned his chair back around and fixed his associate with a piercing, direct gaze. "But you're going to tell me that what you have in that envelope is different."

"I *am* going to tell you that," Marshall returned quietly. "And not only that, Joel. I'm about to say something to you that we've both made fun of people for saying, but here it is: I'm prepared to beg."

Joel's handsome, somber face registered surprise, but he said nothing. He simply sat there, reading Marshall for a moment.

"What is it, exactly, that you're begging for, Marshall?"

"Only that you listen. I'm not asking for any kind of commitment or promise. Only that you listen. Not merely hear. But listen. Really listen. That's all I'm asking."

"You're not bringing me someone down on their luck, who's looking to break into music to get back on the rails, are you, Marshall?"

"She's hardly down on her luck. She doesn't need money," he returned, deciding not to mention that she not only purchased the Emmons estate, but paid cash for it.

"Ah. Spoiled daddy's girl."

"She has no family, at all. You don't know her, Joel, so maybe hold off on the foregone conclusions!" Marshall hadn't meant to bark at him, but he resented having someone talk about Meredith in this way. "I'm sorry," he offered, after Joel crossed his arms and treated him to a mute stare. "It's just that if you knew Meredith Clark, and you heard someone else say things like that about her, you wouldn't like it, either."

"And how is it that you happen to know Miss Clark?" Joel prodded.

"I met her at church, one Sunday morning. Perry introduced her to me. She's been doing spec work at the studio."

"Oh, that's just great," Joel muttered. "If she has money to pay for sessions, and Perry's recording her for free, how big of a stretch is it, to figure out that she's just some beauty queen that he's apparently smitten with? No thanks."

Marshall gaped at him, with a blend of shock and anger. "You know Perry Mitchell better than that!"

"Well, then why is he letting her do spec work?" Joel demanded, not bothering to hide his irritation.

"Because she's worth the risk!" Marshall declared, a little louder than he meant to. "Joel, she's been singing at the homeless shelter, the church's coffeehouse and anywhere else I've been able to book her, all for free, and if you have any questions at all about her, and you can't take my word for it, as much as you say you respect me, then talk to Gary Brenner about her. She actually ministers! She's not afraid to get her hands dirty, Joel, and the response from the people is just indescribable!"

"Try," he said dryly, and Marshall blew out a breath of frustration.

"They crowd around her, just wanting to tell her what her songs mean to them. We've seen a lot of young girls run up to her, crying their eyes out. She listens to them, she bends her head down to really hear them, and then looks them straight in their eyes, holding their hands and praying with them. She will literally stay after a concert all night, until anyone who wants to, gets to speak with her."

"So the response from the people is not so indescribable, after all," Joel commented blandly, casting a pointed look in Marshall's direction.

Marshall just hung his head, weary of sparring with him, but looked back up quickly when Joel suddenly said, "Leave it. I'll listen, maybe tonight. But that's all I'll commit to."

Joel let himself in his front door, and literally allowed everything in his arms to fall to the floor. He didn't care. He made his way over to his sofa and dived onto it with a thud.

Today had been a year long, and just when he thought he could maybe wrap things up early and get out of the office, a contract dispute landed on his desk.

He raised one arm and rested the back of his hand on his forehead and stared up at the ceiling at nothing, then tried closing his eyes, hoping to doze off, but his brain was in high gear and was having none of that.

He finally dragged himself up to a sitting position and wondered if the effort to make dinner was even worth it. The blinking of the phone began to pester him about messages and he grimaced. "Not likely," he muttered darkly and got up to move into the kitchen.

He stood staring into the fridge, moved over to inspect the freezer, then opened the door to his pantry, with nothing appealing to him.

He finally threw some butter into a sauce pan, added rice and browned it, then threw in some spices and broth and let it simmer while he headed back out to see what the paper boy had aimed at today. "Ah, he accidentally hit my porch," he mused. "Maybe he'll improve and get it up on my roof again. Practice makes perfect."

Joel wandered back in, deliberately not looking at his phone, and tossed the paper onto the kitchen table, before plating the pilaf he'd made and bringing it over to eat while he skimmed the headlines. He was a little more hungry, now that he could actually smell it.

He ended up tossing the paper into the trash, without reading it, as he did most evenings, cleared away his dishes and headed back through the living room. A hot shower and hitting the sack sounded promising.

He stopped and wondered if he was just tired, or if the phone's message light suddenly blinked more urgently. Joel let out a mumbled oath and decided to get it over with.

He listened to the first few words of each message, before either fast-forwarding or just deleting.

"Joel!" He recognized Marshall Edwards' voice. "So, what'd you think? Did you hear it, yet? Give me a call, I'm at the house!"

"Oh, crap, I forgot all about that." He blew out a loud breath and went over to where he'd dropped everything, and fished the large envelope out of his briefcase, then took it with him up to his room.

"This better be good, Edwards," he muttered.

He let the CD slide out of the envelope and left everything else in it. He popped it into his player, then stepped into his bathroom to get ready to take his shower. His intention was just to let the CD play in the background but his conscience got the better of him.

Marshall Edwards didn't ask for much. All he had requested today was for Joel to really listen. Marshall was wrong, if he thought Joel didn't respect him.

He let a flash of irritation wash over his face, but dutifully came back to rest on the side of his bed and began playing the tracks.

Joel drew in his breath and closed his eyes, as the anointing that rested on the music began to fill the room. There were only four tracks on the demo, but he simply replayed them when they were done, listening over and over. There was something so familiar about this voice, but Joel knew that if he'd ever heard it before, he wouldn't have to wonder. Still, there was some quality that reached out to him, as if singling him out, as if this was the moment in time these songs had been captured for.

Joel finally stopped the CD, and just sat there. He knew the envelope probably contained a promo pack, but he didn't feel the need to see bios and pictures. In fact, he didn't want to know about anything, but the music.

He picked up the phone by his bed, not wasting time to wander back downstairs to see if his cell phone was in his briefcase, and dialed Marshall's number and, of course, he answered immediately.

"Tomorrow, at four, Marshall."

"Tomorrow!"

"Is that a problem?"

"Not at all!" Marshall made a gesture of celebration and his wife grinned over at him.

"Perhaps you'd better check with Miss Clark, first," Joel pointed out, dryly.

"Oh, don't you worry about Miss Clark! Miss Clark will be there, if I have to hogtie her!"

Joel laughed quietly and hung up, before deciding that if anyone deserved a hot shower and a good night's sleep, it was him and he was going to have it.

When he was finally ready to get into bed, he simply put the player on loop and let the CD play softly, as he drifted off to sleep.

Chapter Twenty-Three

Perry Mitchell swiveled his chair around and gave Meredith an angry scowl. "You can *not* be serious!"

She matched his scowl with one of her own. "Why can't I be?"

"Meredith Clark, I just wanna smack you right now, and, just to be clear, I'm not talking about kissing!" He was actually glaring at her. "If you a guy, I'd box your ears!"

"Don't let that stop you!" she returned, crossing her arms and narrowing her eyes at him.

"Why, in the world, would you come this far, and then, just when we'd all but given up hope that Joel Etheridge would ever give you a shot, you score an appointment with him, and then waltz in here telling me you don't think you'll go? Have you lost your mind?"

Perry was more than a little aggravated. "If you won't do it for yourself, do it me. Do it for Marshall and Bobbie, and Pastor Gary. Heck, do it for Mick! We all believe in you, Meredith, and we've all gone to bat for you. Why now, of all times, would you suddenly get cold feet and decide you're not going? Do you have any idea of what Marshall had to go through to get you in the door?"

She had already said all these things to herself, and hearing them from Perry made her feel more badly than ever, but there was just something about meeting Joel

Etheridge that was causing her to feel rattled. She couldn't understand why, and she had been up most of the night talking to Father about it, but He'd given her nothing more than the passage of scripture in Jeremiah that she'd shared with Miss Marcie, just before she found out she had to leave their home. When she read it last night, she began crying, because the last time Father had led her to read it, her entire life was uprooted. What if that happened again?

She just sat there, letting all these thoughts swarm around her, and began blinking back tears.

Perry immediately felt remorse. "I'm sorry, Merry," he offered. "It's not my place to try to strong-arm you into doing something you don't want to do. But I'm just a little frustrated, because I really believe God is calling you to minister to the world, through your music, and I'm afraid you're maybe letting the enemy steal that from you."

She hung her head and sat silently.

Perry let out a sigh of regret. "I feel like a jerk," he mumbled.

"That's because you *are* a jerk," his friend confirmed, then glanced up at him with a little smile. "I don't know what it is I'm afraid of, Perry. I just am."

"But no one's making you sign anything. It's just a meeting. Well... that's not exactly true. If Joel Etheridge agrees to see an artist he doesn't already know, then he's heard the artist's music and likes what he's heard and, believe me... he generally hates what's brought to him. If he gave you an appointment, it means something about your music has finally reached through to him. That's huge, Merry."

"I guess." She pressed her lips together and stared at the floor.

"Is there something you're not telling me?" Perry asked, furrowing his brow and studying her. "You seem to be keeping something back."

"If I am, I'm not conscious of it," she said softly. "I'm just afraid, but I'm not sure why."

"Well, let me ask you this," he proposed, leaning forward to get her to focus on him. "Does Father generally use fear to guide you?"

She shook her head. "He never has, before."

"Then why should He use it, now? That's obviously not His way, with you, or with any of His children. Why would God use an ungodly motivator? He uses love and grace and mercy and compassion, but why would He pick up a stick of fear and drive you with it, instead of letting the Holy Spirit lead you? It's like Pastor Gary says, God loves us into His kingdom, He doesn't scare us into it. If it's not Him, then that just leaves one culprit. Merry, I really do think the enemy is trying to stop you and he's more than happy to use fear to do it."

She continued to sit quietly, and weigh his words.

"Let's listen." Perry fired up one of Meredith's most recent tracks. "Pay attention to your own words."

Here's my life. You can take it, if You like.
Here's my heart. You can break it if You like.
All my hopes and dreams are anchored in You.
How would I survive without You?

I will walk with You
No matter where You are going,
For I have found in You
There is a peace, there is a knowing,
This world will never understand me like You do,
So I will walk with You.

I was losing in trade.
All the world could give was just a token.
I had to pay,
And promises made were promises broken.
I've come away.

I will walk with You
No matter where You are going,
For I have found in You
There is a peace, there is a knowing,
This world will never understand me like You do,
So I will walk with You.

Perry stopped the track and turned to give his friend a look of compassion. "I know you're afraid, Merry. But you told me that your greatest desire is to be a friend of God. If that's true, then you don't ask Him to walk with *you*. You walk with *Him*.

"Besides, Joel Etheridge loves God as much as anyone I know. I expect God considers him to be His friend, as well. So, if you really mean it when you say 'I will walk with You', then, if Father's going to walk into that meeting with Joel Etheridge today, maybe you should tag along."

Delores looked up from her desk with a sweet smile of welcome and stood as Marshall introduced her to Meredith. She surprised Meredith by coming around her desk and giving her a warm hug.

"Here's that beautiful girl with the beautiful voice!" She looked over at Marshall with joy on her face. "I got to listen to that CD this morning."

"Oh, did you?" The surprise in Marshall's voice was also on his face. That was very unlike Joel.

"I did, and if he doesn't give me my own copy of it, I'm getting Perry on the phone and begging." She laughed and gestured toward the seating area.

"Why don't you both get comfortable? Joel somehow managed to get stuck on a conference call he wasn't expecting, but he's keeping an eye on the clock, so I'm sure he'll get out of that as soon as he can manage it."

She beamed down at Meredith, as she took a seat. "Would you like some coffee or anything else, honey?"

"A little water, please?"

Delores questioned Marshall with her eyes.

"I'm good, Dee."

Normally, Meredith would have made her way straight over to any coffee pot and dived in, but she decided she was jittery enough, without adding caffeine into the mix. She sat now, just sipping her water, then breathing in deeply, and exhaling slowly.

"May I..." She glanced up apologetically. "Is there a ladies' room?"

"Absolutely!" Delores showed her to the door. "And just take your time, sweetie. There's no rush."

She seemed to know how Meredith was feeling, and her easy-going manner helped put her at ease.

Delores returned to her desk and gave Marshall Edwards a wide-eyed look. "That is the most beautiful girl I have ever seen!" she said, in somewhat of a stage whisper.

"Actually, Dee, that's the one thing that has me worried," Marshall admitted, getting up from his chair to sit closer to hers. "Usually, if someone introduces Joel to a beautiful woman, he goes cold."

"Well, Marshall, that's normally because someone is trying to fix him up with one of those women, but that's not the case, here, and Joel knows it," she reassured him. "He laid that CD on my desk today, and I was shocked. When has he ever done that?"

He shook his head. "Never, that I know of." He glanced at his watch. "I guess, if he saw Meredith's picture and still wants to meet with her, he doesn't suspect me of matchmaking, and this really is all about the music, so hopefully, he won't give her any attitude."

Delores looked confused. "He didn't see her picture."

This time, it was Marshall who was bewildered. "It was in the promo pack."

"I asked him about her this morning, what her bio says, what she looks like, all that. He said he just took the CD out and played it but that he never took anything else out of the envelope."

"You mean..." Marshall gestured toward Joel's door. "Do you mean to tell me that Joel Etheridge has no idea what Meredith Clark looks like?"

Delores shook her head. "That's what he said."

A slow smile found its way across Marshall's face and Delores began to smile, herself.

"Oh, this hardly seems fair," she laughed.

"Well, that's one way of looking at it, Dee," Marshall Edwards commented. "Another way would be that this is payback."

They both laughed and Dee picked up the phone.

"Right away," she said, then hung up and motioned toward Joel's door. "He actually wants to talk to you, first, Marshall, so you can go on in and test the waters, and I'll bring Meredith in, when he sends for her."

"Sounds good. Thanks, Dee."

Marshall gave a quick tap, then opened the door and stepped inside.

Joel looked up with a little grin, holding up a folder he'd been working on, and going to great lengths to put it far out of reach, before resting his forearms on his desk and folding his hands nicely and attentively.

"I appreciate that!" Marshall laughed and took a seat. "Thank you, Joel, for doing this."

"Well, I've not done anything yet, but I want to at least meet the person behind the music and determine what else is there."

"Dee said you let her hear the CD this morning," Marshall commented.

"I did. I thought she'd enjoy it," Joel said with a shrug.

"She also said you didn't check out any of the promo material?"

"I did not. This is either about the music, or it's not."

Marshall nodded slowly. "I guess."

"What is it?" Joel asked bluntly.

"Well, I mean... that's what promo packs are for."

"You gave me her music. Again, that's what this is about, isn't it?"

Marshall nodded.

"And it's hers, right? This is all original music?"

"It's all hers," Marshall acknowledged, and decided to let it go.

"What's she expecting to happen, today, Marshall?"

He looked taken aback. "What do you mean?"

"What is it she wants? I don't know how to ask more plainly than that."

"Wouldn't you rather hear that from her?"

Joel looked away toward the windows and let a brief smile flit across his face. "Perhaps that's best," he said quietly. "If she ever decides to join us."

He swiveled his chair back to rest his eyes on his friend. "Marshall, if you don't mind, I'd like her to come in alone, first. I'll have Dee bring you back in, in a few minutes."

Marshall knew this practice was typical for Joel, so he thought nothing of it, but gave him a little grin and headed back out to see if Meredith had returned to the waiting area.

Meredith stood in front of the large mirror in the ladies' room and stared at herself with wide eyes, as if she were a stranger. What was she doing here?

She studied her reflection, not really seeing her beautiful, luminous eyes, her flawless skin, her long, lovely hair that tumbled down to her waist. She did, however, note the flush of pink on her cheeks and the terrified expression on her face.

"Like a deer in headlights," as Miss Marcie would say.

Suddenly, it all became very comical to her and she began to laugh at herself.

"What's the worst that can happen?" she reasoned. "If he doesn't want to help you, you can just go back to your wonderful house and your awesome cat and no harm, no foul. If he does, then you can just see where that road leads you."

She continued to critique herself for another long moment before looking up. "I'm sorry, Father. I know You love me and that You'll never leave me."

"That's right, child," He whispered.

Her face lit up. He had been quiet the past few days, but He was here! Here... in the ladies' room?

That thought made her giggle and then she had to lean over the sink and try to stop laughing. "I'm sorry, Father," she gasped, in an effort to get it together.

She felt His smile and when she came back out into the waiting area, there was a light in her countenance and a peace resting on her that wasn't there, before.

Delores smiled up at Meredith from her desk and stood up to escort her into Joel's office.

She looked over at Marshall curiously and he gave her a little wink.

"He generally likes to meet an artist alone, for the first few minutes, Merry. I'll be right on in."

"I'm counting on it," she laughed, and came over to where Delores was waiting.

She had expected Joel Etheridge's secretary to lead her on into the office and introduce her, but Delores merely opened the door, gave her an encouraging smile, and pulled the door to quietly, after Meredith stepped in.

Joel had assumed that Delores would buzz him, before sending Meredith Clark into his office and, since she also hadn't knocked, but had simply opened his door and then closed it, he was unaware that anyone had entered. Now, as he often did, he sat staring vacantly out the huge wall of windows.

Meredith lifted her hand to her heart, and drew in a quick breath, as her recent dream of being approached by a man while she sat among the grasses in Father's field, suddenly came rushing back to her. The words he'd spoken to her resonated from somewhere deep inside: "Father told me I'd find you here."

She hadn't seen the man's face clearly in the dream, and she could only see Joel's striking profile now, but his wealth of unkempt curls made her think of that man, who came wandering through Father's field, looking for her, whose untamed locks gently moved in the breeze.

A strange, unexpected blanket of peace wrapped itself around Meredith and she knew that Father had come to this meeting. After a moment, she spoke.

"You have clean windows."

It was the voice that Joel Etheridge had all but fallen in love with, and he smiled quietly to himself before turning to look up at a woman who immediately arrested him.

"I don't clean them myself, but thank you."

It was the voice of the man who had spoken to her in her dream, and Meredith's heart began to race.

Joel stood to come around his desk and greet her, tall, and backlit by the bright daylight streaming in behind him through the clean windows, and Meredith needed no more evidence to realize that Father had already introduced them.

They stood there, silently recognizing each other.

"Convention requires me to say 'Hello, Meredith, I'm Joel Etheridge', and to take your hand," he said quietly.

"Etiquette compels me to yield to convention," she returned, smiling up at him.

She offered her hand and Joel captured it with his own.

Intense blue eyes searched tender gray ones and, in the flash of an instant, a lifetime of conversations passed between them.

Chapter Twenty-Four

Growing up, Meredith never had a best friend, but all that changed when she met Hailey Fisher. She had actually met Hailey on a plane in first class, when she had to fly back and forth, from Nashville to St. Louis a few times, to meet with the attorney over some tax matters and loose ends, following the purchase of her home.

Hailey approached her to ask if she'd like anything to drink or to read. Meredith had glanced up to decline, and instantly liked the friendly flight attendant, and had managed to have several small chats with her, throughout the flight's duration, especially after discovering that she also lived in Nashville. Following that first encounter, it seemed that Hailey was a flight attendant on every one of those trips and it became a joke as to who was stalking who.

When she spotted Hailey at Covenant Fellowship one Sunday morning, she made a beeline for her and gave her a big hug.

"Is this *your* church?" she demanded.

"Is it yours?" Hailey countered, with a little laugh.

"Okay, that's it," Meredith decided. "We're obviously meant to be besties."

Today, Meredith's bestie sat curled up on one end of Meredith's couch, while she nested on the other end, and watched Hook's bid for attention with a little laugh.

"So that head-butting thing he's doing to you is really a sign of affection, then?"

"Well, that's what he wants me to think," Meredith said, with a little eye roll. "But, loosely translated, it means for me to either feed him, scratch him, or get off his couch."

Hailey continued to watch the big gray cat work the room with a smile of amusement, before she stretched her arm forward and found a throw pillow to hug.

"The last time I talked to you, you were gonna meet with a record label guy. Did that already happen?"

Meredith coaxed Hook to hop down and go amuse himself elsewhere, before she answered. "Did it ever!"

Hailey shifted her position to sit up straighter. "Oh, this sounds promising! Let's hear it."

"Well, on the surface, there's not much to hear, but you know me. There's always something else going on, below the surface."

They both giggled and Meredith's face took on a more serious expression.

"The short story is that I'm signed, now, to the label. It's not just a label, though. His firm oversees an artist's entire career, including recording, management, booking, public relations... all of it."

"Wow, Merry, that's a lot of power to hand over." Hailey was concerned, and didn't bother to hide it.

"It is, and normally, I would have balked big time, at just handing over the reins like that to someone I just met, but on the other hand, I already knew him."

Hailey widened her expressive brown eyes. "How? Where you did you meet him before?"

"In a field."

Meredith had to laugh at her friend's reaction. "Okay, promise not to make fun of me."

Hailey quickly crossed her heart and waited in suspense.

"I dreamed him."

She opened her eyes even wider. "Shut up!"

"I did, seriously."

"You dreamed him, before you ever met him?"

"I did. I mean, I didn't know who he was, in the dream."

"Tell me the dream," Hailey insisted. "I love hearing other people's dreams!"

"Well, there was this place I stayed for a while, on a farm, before I came to Tennessee."

Her friend nodded.

"When I was there, I spent every minute I could out in one of the fields. That's where I would talk to Father and He would talk back. It'll probably always be my favorite place on the earth.

"So, right before Marshall Edwards was able to get Joel to listen to my music and get me into his office to meet with him, I dreamed about that field. I was sitting in it, and I remember being very content and peaceful. I always felt that way, in the field."

"It sounds amazing," Hailey breathed.

"Oh, Hailey, I wish you could see it, sometimes." Meredith immediately felt the same old rush of tears that crowded into her eyes as she thought about her time in Grayson. "It has tall golden grasses, and Queen Anne's lace, and there's a stream running through it. Well, it's called a branch. If Heaven was a field like that, I wouldn't be disappointed."

She smiled through watery eyes. "So anyway... in the dream, I was sitting in the tall grasses and I had my eyes closed, like I always did, listening to the sounds and smelling the grasses. I heard someone moving toward me, through the grass."

Hailey gasped and hugged her pillow tighter. "This is starting to sound like a nightmare!"

Meredith laughed. "No, it wasn't like that. I remember once really hearing that sound in the field, and it was the first time Father talked to me. That's what I thought in the dream, too. I thought that Father was coming to talk to me.

"But then, there was something blocking the sun from my face and when I opened my eyes, there was a man. He was standing, looking down at me and the sun was so bright behind him, that I couldn't see his face, but he had curly hair and it was sort of moving around in the breeze and then he spoke to me, and it was such a beautiful voice, Hay!"

Hailey began to feel a little shiver of excitement.

"His voice was deep, and comforting and... well, just beautiful. He only said one thing. 'Father told me I'd find you here.' Then he held out his hand and I reached up and took it and when I raised up to stand next to him, I almost saw his face, but then I woke up."

Hailey dropped her head and moaned. "No!" She lifted her face up and looked at Meredith in playful agony. "Are you kidding me, you woke up? Right then, of all times? No, I hate that! Go back and change it!"

Meredith laughed and reached over to swat her arm. "Wait, I'm not done!"

She pulled her long hair out of her eyes and moved around to sit cross-legged, before continuing.

"So, I was confused, of course, but the more I thought about the dream, the more I began to obsess over it, so I made myself put it out of my mind.

"Then, when Marshall told me that I was going to be meeting with the label owner, something in me just panicked. I told Perry Mitchell, my producer, that I didn't think I would go, after all, and he got really mad at me. I don't blame him. Anyway, he's actually the one who talked me into going through with the meeting."

Hailey waved a hand through the air. "Okay, now, this whole conversation started right after you told me you had already met him, in a field. But you said you didn't see his face, so how does that work?"

Meredith smiled faintly to herself, remembering. "Well, his secretary opened the door and I thought she was coming in with me, to introduce us, but she just closed the door behind me and left me standing there."

Hailey drew her brows and let out a sound of surprise. "On purpose?"

"I guess so," Meredith replied. "It just all happened so quickly. But the thing is, he was just sitting there at his desk, with his chair turned to the side, and looking out his windows. He has this huge wall of windows and I guess, if I had to be in an office all day long, I'd be looking out windows, too."

"So, he didn't even notice you?"

"Well, he thought he was still alone. So I had a moment to look at him. He has curly hair..." She broke off and grinned at Hailey's excited little finger clapping.

"All of a sudden, instead of being nervous, I just felt this peace, like everything was just as it should be. So, I said, 'You have clean windows.' That's when he looked over at me and said, 'I don't clean them, myself, but thank you.' And, Hailey, it was *his* voice... the man in the field!"

"Are you sure?" Hailey looked delighted. "For real?"

Meredith nodded, her eyes shining. "Then he stood up."

Hailey gasped. "Please tell me he's tall."

"He's tall."

She bounced up and down on her end of the couch. "I love this story!" she chanted happily.

"Well, it was almost dreamlike, the way it was playing out, there in his office, because when he stood up, he was between me and all the windows that were behind him, and it was really bright, so I couldn't see his face, either, for a moment, until he came around to stand in front of me."

Hailey produced a comical pantomime of beating her heart with one hand and fanning her face with the other. "This is better than a movie!" she declared. "What happened next?"

Meredith laughed at her antics. "Well, not a lot, after that. I mean, he introduced himself and we shook hands. Marshall came in not long after, and we sat for about an hour, talking about where to go from there.

"Anticlimax," Hailey grumbled, with a little pout. "So, no big, sweeping romance, then?"

"Oh, no... he's not... I mean, I took the dream to mean that he would be the one Father would use to help me move forward where He's taking me, but Joel Etheridge is pretty much all business."

Hailey pulled her knees up to her chest and wrapped her arms around them. "Have you met with him, since then?"

"I have to meet with him all the time, lately. He's officially my manager."

Meredith's friend seemed to think this was odd. "If he's head honcho over there... wait..." Her face took on a look of astonishment. "Wait... Etheridge? As in Etheridge and Associates?"

Meredith looked at her oddly. "Of course. Who else did you think I meant?"

"No, but..." Hailey just sat and stared at her. "You really don't know who he is?"

"I mean..." Meredith seemed lost as to what it was Hailey was expecting her to say. "He owns the firm."

"Merry!" Hailey crossed her arms and just looked at her. "You really don't watch any TV or keep up with the news around this city, do you?"

Meredith shrugged. "I'm just not into television, I guess."

"And it shows!" Hailey was amazed that Meredith had no idea who her manager was. "Honey, Joel Etheridge has won just about every industry award there is! Etheridge and Associates is forever scoring yet another feat of recognition in the music industry! Even someone like me, who has no connection at all to that world, knows who Joel Etheridge is! And you're sitting here, telling me that he, himself, is managing your career, instead of having one of his staff assigned to you? Seriously?"

Meredith shrugged again. "I guess so. I mean, Joel Etheridge is my manager."

Hailey just sat there, looking at her and shaking her head. "So... no sparks flying between the two of you, then? He's just all about your career?"

Meredith looked down with a little flush. "He just reminds me of Father, a little bit, so that's probably why I feel such a strong connection to him."

"You feel a strong connection?" Hailey seized on that. "Are you sure he's not feeling a strong connection, as well? Because, Merry, according to what I've read and heard, Joel Etheridge doesn't manage anyone. He pays people to handle all that for him. He's obviously making an exception, in your case. He wouldn't just do that, for no reason."

Meredith studied her for a quiet moment. "Well, to be honest, Hailey... sometimes, I think there's a little moment, like when he's talking to me and instead of looking at my eyes, he's looking into them, if that makes sense. But, it's probably my imagination and even if it wasn't, I can't let myself be affected by that. I don't plan to ever let a man get close to me again." She frowned sadly. "But, like I said, Joel Etheridge is pretty much all business, so I'm able to relax and not worry about getting too close. I imagine he's already in a relationship, anyway."

"Oh, I seriously doubt it. No woman is going to stand idly by, and let her significant other be linked to a woman who looks like you. No offense," Hailey laughed. "I only know him by sight, because of who he is, but when he's at church, all the women seem to suddenly find a chair in his section, and he's completely oblivious to any of them. I doubt seriously that he even makes time for a relationship. It's a shame, too."

Meredith glanced up at her. "Why do you say that?"

"Hello!" Hailey belted out a little laugh. "Have you *seen* that man?"

Meredith grinned. "Well, I guess we all have to have a face," she speculated.

"Well, God sure enough handed *that* man a face, let me tell you!" Hailey bopped Meredith with the pillow. "But He sure enough handed *you* a face, too, which is why I'm surprised he's able to keep things strictly platonic. I wonder how long he'll be able to keep that up?" she mused softly, to herself.

Chapter Twenty-Five

Joel Etheridge pulled his car through the gates of Meredith's property, scowling to himself, annoyed that the gates were not only unlocked, but wide open, and that he was able to breeze right through. He pulled around to the front of the house, and sat a moment, rifling through some papers in his briefcase, before satisfying himself that he'd brought what he needed, and approaching her door to ring the bell.

Her Jeep was there, but she was taking so long to answer, that he began to wonder if she were out on the grounds. She interrupted his speculation by pulling the door open and leaving it that way, without even looking at him, and immediately turning around and heading back out into the kitchen, where her fridge's door stood ajar, while its contents rested on the floor. A ripe odor was taking up residence.

Rather than being amused, this further served to irritate Joel, but he stood quietly, watching her awkward attempts to sort through the mess, with a trash can waiting beside her, in case she needed it to get involved.

He resisted the urge to speak, and remained silent, wondering just how long she would continue to sit on the floor, foraging through potential salmonella, constantly lifting her long hair to one side, to keep it out the food, only to have it tumble back down to the floor, before realizing that she had actually just let someone into her house.

He watched her draw her brows into a frown and open a package of what looked as if it had once been ham. She cautiously sniffed it, made a face, and yelled "Bingo!" before hurling it away.

It landed neatly on Joel's shoe and he glanced down at it, pressing his lips tightly together, and breathing in deeply. Meredith began looking around to see where the offensive lunch meat had landed and saw it, on a shoe, on a foot, on a leg... her eyes traveled upward until they met Joel's, and she put a hand over her mouth to keep from laughing.

Joel was still keeping a running total in his head of all the things he intended to fuss at her about, but he grudgingly smiled, in spite of himself, and lifted the ancient cold cuts off his shoe and flung them into the trash can.

"Is that it?" he asked, nodding toward the trash can, "or have you only just begun unraveling the mystery of that fascinating scent?"

"Oh, you can smell it too, huh?" Meredith grinned.

"I imagine your entire neighborhood can smell it," Joel returned dryly. "Is that it?" he repeated.

"I think so." Meredith started piling everything back into her fridge, then stopped and looked up at him in confusion. "How long have you been here?"

"That is exactly what I want to talk to you about," he answered, with his previous displeasure washing back over his face.

"You want to talk to me about how long you've been here?" She continued to sit among the condiments, looking bewildered.

Joel came over to crouch down and help put the rest of the food back where it belonged, solely in the interest of time.

"In a manner of speaking." He stood up and reached his hand down to her. "Up."

Meredith quickly squashed the flashback of her dream, and obediently let him help her to her feet. She looked back at the trash can, before turning to him with a question in her eyes.

"Do you have any zip lock bags in the utility room?" he asked, gesturing in that direction.

She nodded, but made no attempt to go find them. Neither did Joel.

"When I leave, go get one and put that stinking mess in it and seal it up, until you can get the trash taken out. "

He turned to move back out to Meredith's living room and she slowly followed him, with an apathetic shrug.

Joel motioned toward the couch. "Have a seat, Merry, I want to run over a few things with you."

"Why does it sound like you want to run over *me*, with a few things?" she muttered, half under her breath, and Joel was unable to hide a little smile.

"I had intended to just talk about this California thing, and we'll still have that talk, but first..." He sat down on the edge of the large coffee table so that he could face her.

"I have chairs, Joel," she said, with a touch of sarcasm.

"This is fine." He studied her for a moment, until she began to feel a little self-conscious.

"Meredith, why are your gates wide open?"

She leveled her beautiful gray eyes at him. "Is that a metaphor?   Or an analogy?   I always get those mixed up."

He nodded out toward the front of her property.

"Oh, my gates! So, my actual gates, then."

Joel narrowed his eyes. "What did you think I meant?"

She grinned and made no reply.

"Those gates are there for a reason," Joel continued, "and I'd like for you to keep them closed and locked, please."

"It's a hassle," she protested. "It's much easier to just zip in and out without having to wait for the gates."

"How much of a hurry are you in, that you can't factor ten seconds into your day, to accommodate the gates?" Joel lifted his hand to stop her from arguing that all those ten seconds added up, and fixed her with a stern look.

"You opened the front door and walked off, without even looking up to see who was here. You literally just let me walk on into your house, Meredith! I could have been anybody!" He was not pleased.

She had already gotten to know Joel Etheridge well enough to recognize that he was not in a kidding mood, and if she continued to make light of things, he very well might lose it. He'd never yelled at her before, but according to his reputation, he was a legend, in that regard.

She leaned back into the couch cushions and crossed her arms in a little sulk, resting her bare feet on the table beside him. "What else?"

He glanced down at her feet, then lifted his eyes to hers.

"Oh, you have got to be kidding me!" Meredith exclaimed. "I'm in my own home, Joel! You're not seriously ordering me to go get some shoes on?"

"What you do, or do not have on your feet in the privacy of your own home is of no concern to me."

"Well, hallelujah!" she began, but he flashed her a look that checked the rest of her comeback.

"What you do, or do not have on your feet, when you are in public or onstage, however, *is* of concern to me."

She continued to sit with her arms crossed in defiance, glowering at him.

"Meredith, I'm not kidding," he said quietly.

"Oh, I know. You're far too gripey to be kidding."

Joel Etheridge had never had anyone respond to him so recklessly before, and he leaned forward and locked his disturbing blue eyes onto hers.

"I gave you a pass after your last concert, because it was pointed out to me that I had neglected to make you aware of my policy regarding how you are expected to dress for a performance, even though it is clearly spelled out in your contract... a document, I am beginning to suspect, that you've never bothered reading."

"I used it to fix a wobbly table," she grumbled, shooting him a look of belligerence.

Joel let out a loud sigh, wondering whatever made him think he had either the time or the patience to work with this beautiful, difficult, exasperating woman.

"I suggest you call a handyman about your table and actually take the time to read something that you were so willing to sign your name to," he said, calmly but firmly. He continued to rest his eyes on hers.

"Meredith, the next time you show up in concert barefoot, in your old blue jeans and cut off sweatshirts, or any such attire, I will personally walk out and pack you off that stage like a twenty pound sack of dog food."

She stopped herself, just in time, from asking if it could be cat food instead, but still grinned to herself, imagining what his response would be.

Meredith looked up quickly as she felt Joel's hand on her bare foot. He lifted it slightly and allowed the very faintest ghost of a smile to cross his lips. "This, while quite lovely, making an appearance outside this house, violates your contract. Are we clear?"

"What about the other one?" She was equally divided between being mad at Joel and showing him to the door, or engaging in a game of witty banter. She was convinced she would enjoy either one.

"The other one is also quite lovely," he replied, with a solemn expression on his handsome face, betrayed only by the slightest sparkle in his eyes, "but showing your audience just how lovely is unacceptable."

"But Joel..." Meredith looked at him with a seriousness in her eyes that caused him to pay attention. "I have to play the piano barefoot."

He studied her for a moment, waiting for her to smile, but the smile never came. She was authentically worried.

"Why?" He waited.

"I don't know, it's just... it's part of how I play. I can't explain it, but if I'm wearing shoes, I'll hit all kinds of clams. I'm being serious, Joel." Her eyes backed up her claim.

"I'm willing to agree to your slipping off your shoes, while at the piano, Merry, provided you don't enter the stage or leave the stage barefoot. Are we agreed?"

She smiled so brilliantly that it almost took his breath away.

The sun was unusually bright and hot at the outdoor rally in Southern California and Meredith kept lifting her long mane of hair up off her neck and shielding her eyes with one hand.

Everyone out in the crowd either had umbrellas over them to produce some shade, or were fanning themselves with whatever they could find to create a little breeze.

When the emcee introduced her, she came out onto the stage in a tank top, jeans, and sandals and stopped at the emcee's mic to greet the audience before taking her place at the piano.

Just as she'd begun speaking, a murmur began to ripple through the crowd and they all began looking toward the direction Meredith had just come from. She glanced over to see what was causing all the commotion, just before she was lifted up into the air, slung over Joel Etheridge's shoulder, and carried off the stage. The crowd began cheering and applauding at what they assumed was a gimmick, but Joel was neither cheering, nor applauding.

"Introduce the next act," he gritted out to the emcee, and continued on to the RV parked behind the stage, with Meredith still balanced on his shoulder, too shocked to struggle or demand to be put down.

Joel opened the door to the RV and easily stepped up with his light load, closing the door behind them, before placing her on her feet and lifting a finger to warn her not to start up with him.

"I do not make idle threats," he said, in a low, controlled voice. "Don't test me again, Meredith."

"I wasn't testing you, I was trying to wear something I could breathe in! It's a hundred degrees out there, Joel! I don't see what difference it makes, anyway. I was just blending in with everybody else."

"You were given plenty of options, and in plenty of time, to be able to come up with something that would allow you to breathe and still be appropriate. You were warned."

"I swear, you hate me," she whispered, hanging her head to keep him from seeing the tears she felt coming.

Joel came close and put a finger under her chin, forcing her to look up at him. "Why would you say something like that?" he demanded. "Is that really what you think?"

She wouldn't answer and he stood looking down at her with a range of emotions warring for dominance.

"Do you want to go back out there in a bit, and do your set?"

She looked up at him in alarm. "Are you freakin' kidding me? After the way you just humiliated me?"

"Meredith, how can you take no responsibility at all for how this played out?" Joel watched her struggle with his question. "We talked about this, and I thought I'd made myself clear."

"But Joel, I didn't think you'd really come out onto the stage and carry me off."

"I said I would," he reminded her quietly.

They just stood there, Meredith sorry that she had defied him, and Joel sorry that he had made good on his threat, but neither would admit it.

"Come with me," he said suddenly.

"Back out there?" She shook her head.

"No. Not back out there. Come with me."

"You can't just leave the rally!"

"Watch me. Come." He took her hand, persuading her to obey, and led her out to where his rental car was parked, opening her door and allowing her to be seated.

She watched him move around to get in, her face reflecting the curious amazement she was feeling.

"Where are we going?" she asked him, as he checked to see if she was belted in, before pulling out of the parking lot.

"You'll see," he answered lightly, with the flash of a rare grin. "Don't worry," he added, noting her look of concern. "I'm not headed to the border with you, Merry."

She decided that the best thing was to just wait and see, since Joel was clearly not simply going to tell her.

She couldn't mask her surprise when he stopped the car in front of one of Beverly Hills' most exclusive boutiques and handed his keys to the valet, before proceeding with her to the entrance.

She stopped him at the door, looking down at her jeans. "I can't go in there like this," she protested, in a panic.

"I can promise you, Meredith, that when you walk in, they won't be looking at your clothes." Joel tucked her hand under his arm and escorted her into the shop, returning the smile that an attendant was quick to offer him.

"May I be of assistance?" she inquired, her eyes immediately traveling to the striking, beautiful woman, on the arm of one of the most handsome men she had ever seen.

Meredith flashed an uncertain smile at her, then looked up at Joel, her eyes filled with questions.

"You may, indeed," Joel assured her, and the attendant led the way over to a seating area, after determining that Joel wanted Meredith to be shown dresses. He particularly asked for something flowing and in lace, and the attendant soon brought out a black, midi-length dress for the both of them to inspect.

"This is French Leavers lace," she informed him. "Very superior to anything mass produced."

Joel fingered the lace and appreciated its softness and intricate design. "Please take it to the fitting room. I'd like to see it paired with black boots, if that's possible, preferably suede, tall shaft, low heel. Relaxed."

"Of course!" The attendant led a puzzled Meredith into the fitting room and asked for sizes, leaving her to continue pondering why Joel was doing this. She decided that he probably felt bad for the way today went, and was trying to be nice, so she put up no resistance, and allowed the attendant to help her into the dramatic, black dress.

When Meredith also put on the boots the attendant had brought and stood looking at herself in the mirror, her first reaction was to wonder how Joel Etheridge could have been so accurate about what would look good on her.

The attendant beamed into the mirror with approval. "This ensemble was made for you. You're an absolute vision!"

She opened the door and led Meredith back into the seating area, for Joel to see her.

When she came out and stood before him, Joel slowly rose to his feet and his reaction was one of stunned silence. He cleared his throat and struggled to force himself to pull his gaze away from her. His face was unreadable.

He collected himself, and quietly informed the attendant of a sale, as Meredith returned to get dressed to leave the shop.

The drive back to the grounds of the rally was made in silence. After Joel stopped the engine, they both sat, making no attempt to get out of the car, before Meredith finally braved the question.

"Why did you do this, Joel?"

He sat looking at nothing for a moment, before he finally said, "A couple of reasons, one being that I wanted you to realize, Meredith, that you were not created to just blend in. You were created to shine."

She looked down at her hands and allowed a faint smile to paint her lips. She glanced over at him, studying his profile, wondering what thoughts were moving about in his mind, as he idly viewed the parking lot, without seeing it.

"What's the other reason?" she finally asked.

"The other reason," he said, in a soft voice, before looking over to search her eyes with his, "is that I don't hate you, little one."

Chapter Twenty-Six

Meredith stood looking out one of the many windows in her music room, her eyes roaming slowly over the beautiful grounds of her home. She wrapped her arms around herself, in a little hug, and grimaced at her cloudy reflection in the window.

She chided herself for not cleaning the windows in this house, because she did so love the views that it afforded, and all it asked in return was for her to put forth the effort to do a little window washing. She kept meaning to.

Another fall season was again visiting Tennessee. Meredith counted the number of Tennessee autumns she had experienced and her eyes widened with surprise.

She came away from the window with a little sigh. Her thoughts had been returning, all morning, to that glorious time of her life she had spent with the kind, generous, and loving Blake family in Louisiana. It jarred Meredith to realize that Carlyn was now twenty years old!

She'd been delighted to find an email from her, telling her how proud she and her family were of Meredith's success in the music industry and letting Meredith know that she was currently in California and had been doing some recording. She admitted that she wasn't feeling as excited now, as when she'd first traveled there, and asked for her prayers.

Meredith had responded quickly and told Carlyn that if she could ever help her at all, to please let her know right away. She promised to pray and asked Carlyn to be sure to let her parents know how much she loved and missed them.

Meredith knew that thinking too much about her beloved Pastor Fred, Miss Marcie, and her little Carlyn, and the beautiful Father's field would only cause her to break into tears, but she had to give in and follow a few more memories where they led her.

When she thought about her first fishing trip with Pastor Fred and Miss Marcie, her eyes lit up and she rippled out a little laugh, remembering how Miss Marcie had given her a big grin, after she had hopped out of the truck when they were leaving to head back home, and dashed back to the banks of Castor Creek, and then raced back and climbed in, all to Pastor Fred's befuddlement. But what really made Miss Marcie break into stomach-grabbing laughter was when Meredith leaned over and muttered, "It was ringing when it hit the water."

Meredith wiped tears of happy memories out of her eyes, thinking of what pure joy it had given her to actually follow Miss Marcie's admonition to "just fling that thing into the bottom of Castor Creek and be done with all of it."

She missed fishing and admitted this to Joel, a few days ago, when he noticed a little sadness around her eyes. His first thought was that he had put it there, since it took so little effort on his part lately, to put a shadow on her pretty face, or cause her to drop her gaze down to the floor.

When she told him that she was just missing getting to go fishing, Joel immediately arranged to take her, relieved that this wasn't something he had caused, but was something he could easily remedy.

Delores and Marshall had exchanged looks of surprise when Joel had passed through the waiting area, on his way to the elevators, and casually informed them that he wouldn't be in the next day, because he was taking Meredith fishing.

Delores had tried to remind him of a couple of meetings, but if he heard her, he ignored her, and she was forced to call both parties and reschedule.

Meredith had told Joel that she preferred fishing from the banks, but that she had rented a boat in Missouri, to keep from being approached by strangers. He informed her that he was perfectly content to fish from the banks, and that if some guy tried to make her acquaintance, he would only try once.

The thought of finally getting to go fishing filled Meredith with a childlike excitement. She sang out an impromptu, silly little song about catfish, and scooped up Hook, carrying him downstairs under her arm like a football, to help her figure out where she had put her tackle box and rod, so she'd be ready to head out in the morning.

Joel looked down at Meredith as she opened the door, and let out an impatient sigh. "The gates, Merry," he reminded.

"Yes, I like the gates, too," she said, suppressing a little smile and moving back to let him come in.

"Then let them do their job," Joel reasoned, wearily. "They just want to act like real gates, and you're ruining that, for them."

Meredith rolled her eyes and swatted him on the arm. "Oh, stop it, old man Etheridge," she admonished, using Joel's Music Row nickname.

"Funny, how no one ever called me that, until you showed up," he muttered, and she let out a little giggle.

Joel smiled to himself. She was happy. She was going fishing and she was happy. That alone, was starting his day off in a good direction.

He reached down and rumpled Hook's fur, and the big cat immediately began to shove his head against Joel's hand and purr loudly.

"Sorry, Captain Hook," Joel said, straightening up and looking down at him with a little grin. "You have to stay here. It wouldn't be fair to the fish, if you showed up."

Meredith stood looking around thoughtfully, then raised her eyes to Joel, who was standing with his arms crossed, gazing down at her with silent amusement.

"Should I pack us a lunch?" she wondered.

"If you think I'm going to eat anything from that fridge of yours, step back, take a deep breath, and have another shot at thinking," he informed her.

She gave him a little pout and landed another swat.

"What's with all the violence, this morning?" Joel protested lightly. "Come on, Missy, let's go. I took care of lunch."

She grinned at the nickname he'd christened her with. Apparently, she was Missy and Hailey was Sissy. That was what Joel had decided, when they had both sat with him at church and wouldn't quit whispering and giggling. He threatened to sit between them, if they didn't stop.

After church, he'd given Meredith's long tresses a little tug and leaned in to announce to both of them, that since they were acting like little girls, he would be referring to them by their little girl names. He tried to say it with his trademark scowl, but Meredith knew if she stood her ground and waited long enough, his smile would betray him, and it did.

She bent down to give Hook a brief warning about his little boy behavior, then grabbed her jacket and let Joel carry her rod and tackle to her Jeep, since Joel's Cadillac wasn't best suited for stinky fish and muddy trails.

"Keys, please," he demanded. "Hand them over peacefully, Miss Clark."

She sighed and dug them out of her jacket pocket, slapping them into his hand with a grimace.

"You're not my chauffeur," he reminded her. He waited until she was belted in, then pulled the Jeep through the opened gates, pressing the remote on the visor to close them securely behind them.

"See how easy that was?" he teased, glancing both ways before pulling out onto the boulevard.

Joel drove them up to Cedar Hill Lake, which wasn't too far, and had nice areas for bank fishing. It was a weekday and he didn't anticipate much of a crowd.

Fall color was spicing things up early this year, but the sun was warm. Joel pulled the Jeep as closely as he could to the fishing spot he had in mind, then parked it and came around to open Meredith's door. He'd actually had a chance to beat her to it, since she was bent down, putting on the sneakers she'd had in her hands, when she'd left her house in bare feet.

Joel slipped into a large backpack, and grabbed a small ice chest, net, and his own gear, allowing Meredith to carry hers, and led the way over to a clearing, that only appeared once he navigated his way through a stand of trees. The area was completely secluded.

Meredith stood and looked around appreciatively. "How do you know about this place, Joel?"

"It's one of the spots I fish, whenever I actually have time to fish. I used to make time," he added, with a little clench in his jaw.

Meredith was surprised to learn that Joel was something of an outdoorsman. She didn't think it was possible, certainly not with his demanding schedule. She took a covert moment, as he was getting out of his backpack and looking for various things, to study him closely. She'd never seen Joel in anything but a suit and tie, for the most part, or maybe designer jeans and a pullover at church, but certainly not as casually dressed as he was, today. She decided that he looked like a model for some nature magazine, except that his hiking boots were well worn, and both the flannel shirt he had on under his fishing vest, and his jeans were nicely faded and even a little threadbare. She silently approved, and looked away quickly, as he glanced toward her.

"What are we fishing for?" he asked. "They routinely stock this lake with trout and sometimes channel cat."

"I don't know about you, but it's catfish or nothing, for me. I'll throw back a ten pound bass and keep a two pound cat," she said firmly.

Joel flashed her a little grin. "So, you're okay with keeping what you catch, then? Wait, let me guess. Your manager will clean them for you."

She laughed. "Joel, I can skin a cat, don't you worry!"

He looked around at the fall color and grinned, then nodded toward the bank. "Let's see what ya got, girly."

Joel knew all about blood bait, and had some himself, but he'd never seen anyone use little squares of nylon hose to wrap them in.

"That's brilliant," he admitted. "Where'd you learn that trick, Missy?"

"Pastor Fred," she answered, with a beautiful smile, that the memory created.

"You've not talked about him very much," Joel observed. "But when you do, your little face lights up. Maybe you should camp out around memories that do that to you."

"It's hard, though," she confessed, after casting where she wanted, and sitting on a rock to watch her bobber. "Because I miss him so much. I miss that whole family," she added with a sigh.

"So using nylons to wrap blood bait is basic Louisiana wisdom," Joel said lightly, skillfully redirecting the conversation back toward fishing. He'd always noticed that Meredith loved talking about Louisiana, but only when it involved her time with the Blake family. He'd innocently asked her once why she was ever in Louisiana to start with, and her face quickly drained of all color and she hastily changed the subject.

He didn't want that today. Today was just about making her happy.

"Where's your bobber?" he asked, nodding toward her line.

"What? I didn't feel anything!" she exclaimed. "I'm losing my touch, because I'm out of practice," she fussed, hopping up and paying attention to what the fish was doing on the other end of her line. As soon as she felt him moving away, she slowly set the hook and began pulling him in, not playing him too much, but keeping a constant tension on the line.

Joel had picked up the net and came around to the bank to wait for her to land the fish and when it became evident that Meredith wouldn't have to throw this one back, she let out a little whoop of delight.

"He's a beauty," Joel pronounced. "And now, the race is on."

Joel managed to do well, himself, but he enjoyed watching Meredith in her element so much, that he soon laid his rod down and became a spectator. She had finally begun throwing back everything she caught, deciding that they had enough for what Miss Marcie would call a "right good mess".

"So, what's the plan?" Joel asked, when they had cleaned their hands, and relaxed on an old blanket he'd brought to sit on and have lunch. "Are we skinning these bad boys at your place, or mine?"

Meredith looked up at him with excitement. "Are we having a fish fry?"

"Isn't that the point?" he returned, with a little smile.

"Your house, then," she decided. "I'm tired of you making fun of my fridge."

Joel laughed quietly at that. "You're on. Let's just head there, from here, and I'll pick up my car, after."

They finished lunch and then began looking around for whatever needed packing up or throwing into a trash bag and were soon headed back to Joel's beautiful home, which was only a short distance away from Meredith's.

They followed the path around to his back yard, and he opened a shed to retrieve some pliers and sharp knives and before long, they made short work of skinning and filleting their catch. Joel took a shovel out of his shed and dug a hole to bury the remains, grinning at Meredith's curious expression.

"Trust me, it's just easier," he explained. "Consider it fertilizer. Besides, I prefer it over your method of stowing it in the fridge, to corrupt the rest of what's in there, like some kind of science experiment gone wrong." He led the way into the kitchen's back door.

Meredith couldn't resist coaching Joel on the finer points of frying catfish, but perched on a bar stool and allowed him the actual honor. He not only fried them to her high standards, but increased her admiration by whipping up some hushpuppies and tossing a salad.

"Why aren't you married?" she wondered, not realizing she'd spoken out loud.

Joel smiled down into the silverware drawer and collected some forks for them. "Is that a proposal?"

He turned slightly and grinned at her over his shoulder. "Because, if it is, I suspect you have a better one in you than that."

Meredith laughed and stretched her arms up toward the ceiling, with a tired, satisfied yawn. "I'll work on it, and get back to you," she joked.

She balanced on the stool with her elbows on the counter, resting her chin on the palms of her hands, and watching him in silent appreciation.

"You know, you're not scary all the time," she pointed out thoughtfully.

"Don't let that get out," he advised, displaying a playful scowl and narrowing his eyes.

She laughed. "I'm being serious."

"So am I." He brought their plates over to where she was sitting and pulled up a stool next to her. "For all intents and purposes, I am to be feared. Remember that."

She held up a piece of fish to him. He lifted a piece and held it up and they toasted. Meredith was blissfully happy and Joel was peacefully content.

Chapter Twenty-Seven

Meredith half sat and half lay in the window seat, watching the rain running down the pane in tiny, little rivulets. It was a cold, messy rain, the sort that Tennessee was famous for, this time of year.

She eyed it sullenly and glanced over to see if Hook was as displeased with it as she was, but he had already decided it was optimal sleeping weather and was napping hard enough to make little snore noises.

There was plenty that Meredith could be doing, if she were ambitious enough. She had laundry beginning to pile up and she had an unwritten song in her head that just needed to be coaxed out, but she wasn't in the mood for either.

She let her eyes travel over to the large coffee table in front of her couch, and grimaced at the mound of unopened mail and magazines that had been piling up. Joel had fussed at her for creating a fire hazard and, in his own, not so subtle way, suggested that she spend today going through all of it and feeding the shredder with anything she didn't just have to have. She wasn't in the mood for that, either. Besides, he hadn't exactly suggested. He had, more or less, just told her to do it. Meredith was feeling a bit rebellious today though, and was of the firm opinion that it was fine, the way it was.

She let out a loud sigh and raised her eyes up to the wet, dripping limbs of the tree just outside the window. She was lonely. Hailey was working a flight and Perry had a couple of sessions today, so there was no hope for having any fun with either of those two.

She had thought of making up some excuse to call Joel, but of course, he was at the office, probably in meetings, and could be pretty abrupt when someone interrupted him for no good reason. He was much less often the friend who took her fishing, than he was the scowling, impatient manager who seemed to always find something to gripe at her about.

Meredith was striking out, three for three, and beginning to feel sorry for herself.

"Hey, Father," she murmured, in a dull voice, not really expecting a response.

"Hello," He answered and she sat up straighter, as a bright smile instantly lit up her face. Father hadn't spoken to her in a long while. He'd been having her open her Bible for almost everything for so long now, that she'd almost forgotten what it was like to hear His voice any other way.

"Hi!" she said, again. "Where have You been?"

"I think you know the answer to that," He reminded her softly.

She pulled her long hair back to one side and tucked her bare feet up underneath, and smiled up at Him. "You've been right here, I know."

"That's right."

"It's not the same," she said quietly.

"It is the same," He corrected. "You're just being influenced by your feelings."

"What's wrong with that?" she wondered out loud.

"There's nothing wrong or right with feelings," He replied. "Feelings are just feelings. You're not to be guided by them, good or bad. Your feelings will tell you that you're all alone, but I have told you differently. Your feelings will lie to you, as often as they will tell you the truth. But I've told you in My word and in your ear that I will never leave you, regardless of how you feel."

Meredith considered that for a few minutes. "I've missed You," she whispered, after a while.

"Why?"

She was surprised. It wasn't the sort of thing one usually asked. "What do You mean?"

"Why have you missed Me?"

She grinned. "You want me to remember that there's no reason to miss someone who is right here."

"That's right."

"But like right now, Father... this feels more like our time in the field together. It feels like the beginning."

"We're not at the beginning," He said softly. "You said you would walk Me, no matter where I am going. We can't stay at the beginning."

"I wish we could," she sighed.

"No. You just think you do. It feels familiar and safe, so you want to just stay in the field. But if you will walk with Me, you must go where I am going."

"Where are You going?" she wondered, a bit nervously.

"Come and see," He whispered.

Meredith was unaware of the tears that had begun glistening on her cheeks. "But where are we going, Father?" she persisted, looking up anxiously.

"So, you only want to walk with Me, if you know, ahead of time, where We're going?" He waited.

"Child," her Father said, in a voice filled with love and patience, "are you My friend, or are you not?"

Meredith hung her head. Father shouldn't have to ask her that, she told herself. "I hope I am. I want to be," she added, taking a swipe at her cheek.

"Then don't rely on your feelings to tell you whether or not I am with you. I said I would never leave you. But if you don't walk with Me and go where I am going, it will seem to you as if I have. Follow Me."

"How will I know which way You've gone?" she asked quickly, with tears still threatening. "How will I be able to keep up?"

"You will hear My voice behind you. When you turn off the path, to the right or to the left, I will say, 'This is the right way. Walk in it.' I will never leave you, child," He breathed. "I love you. Follow Me."

"I love you, too," she responded, from a full heart.

She leaned her head against the window frame and hugged a pillow tightly. Father seemed to have grown quiet again, and she knew that she was entering into another place of growth where she would have to rely solely on His word to guide her and, for a season, her life would seem less like a walk of faith, and more like a blind groping, but she would just have to stay on the path, regardless of how she felt.

Meredith couldn't explain what was going on with her, today. She just felt like weeping and she didn't understand why. Her ministry and career had skyrocketed, once Joel had begun working with her. She was touring regularly, recording new material with Perry fairly often, and she was in demand for practically every kind of event she could name. Her face was on billboards in every city where she was scheduled to appear, and she was constantly featured on the front cover of every magazine that wrote about her industry.

She had a beautiful home and loving friends. She was financially secure, even after placing almost all of her inherited fortune into the purchase of her house and property, primarily because of the funds that Etheridge and Associates generated for her.

She couldn't understand what, in the world, someone as blessed as she was could possibly have to feel weepy about, and she was beginning to grow cross and impatient with herself.

"Maybe it's just hormones," she muttered dismally.

She pulled her knees up to her chest and rested her arms on them, watching the rain continue to drizzle down the window. She felt the unexpected stirring of something faint, coming from inside her and closed her eyes, quietly singing along with the piano music that drifted into her memory, across the years, from a tiny, little church in the country, in Caldwell Parish.

Why should I feel discouraged?
Why should the shadows come?
Why should my heart be lonely
And long for Heaven and home,
When Jesus is my portion?
My constant Friend is He.
His eye is on the sparrow,
And I know He watches me.
His eye is on the sparrow,
And I know He watches me.

Joel Etheridge sat staring out at the dreary rain that pelted and ran down the windows, painting the city below a gloomy gray. He rose and walked over to the glass to gaze out, feeling a bleakness creep over him. He'd been feeling out of sorts all day, and couldn't seem to shake it off.

He finally ran an impatient hand through his hair and breathed out a muted confession.

"I miss her, Lord. She drives me up the wall and works on my last nerve, but when she's not around, I feel useless."

He smiled wryly at himself. "Maybe it's because no one here is half as much fun to fuss at, as she is."

He breathed in deeply and exhaled slowly, in an attempt to focus on his duties here, and not give in to this strong desire just to see her. Finally, he grabbed his coat and headed out, informing Delores that he was gone for the rest of the day.

It suddenly seemed to him that he couldn't cover the miles quickly enough and when he finally pulled into Meredith's property, he was actually glad that the gates were open. It gave him a reason to gently scold her. He grinned to himself and drove around to stop in front of the house.

The rain was only misting at this point, and he stepped up onto the porch and rang the bell.

A slightly disheveled, teary-eyed Meredith opened the door cautiously, then looked up at him in wonder.

"Your gates are wide open," he said quietly, looking down at her and lifting a strand of wet hair from her cheek.

She stepped back to let him in, as a sad smile rested on her beautiful, tear-streaked face. "Is that a metaphor?"

"It might be," he admitted, with a sigh.

She stood looking up at him, and he returned her gaze for a long moment.

"Are your gates open, Joel?" she asked softly.

"If you need them to be."

He wiped a fresh tear away and studied her with tenderness in his eyes, before opening his arms and wrapping her close in a comforting hug. "Why are you crying, little one?"

"I don't know," she whispered honestly, laying her head against his chest.

"Maybe you're feeling a little overwhelmed?"

"Maybe."

"Well..." Joel let his eyes travel around her lovely home and dwell on the coffee table with its mountain of mail. "I may be able to help with some of that."

She lifted her face to look up at him, then followed his gaze over to the table. She glanced back at him with an embarrassed little grin.

"I was going to get to it."

"Oh, I'm sure," he laughed quietly, relaxing his arms.

She watched the man from the field settle down on the couch, and begin to sort through the pile and a sudden rush of warmth washed over her.

"Joel?"

He glanced up at her, and realized that whatever she had been about to say, she had shied away from, now. He smiled and patted the couch next to him, and she came to rest beside him.

"Let's knock this out first, because we have more pressing things that demand our attention," he said, looking over at her with gentle eyes, and a teasing little smile playing around his lips.

"What kind of things?"

He nodded toward her kitchen.

"Anything but that," she groaned.

"Oh, we're just getting started," he informed her lightly. "I've saved the best for last. You've never had as much fun in your life, as you're going to have, when we start washing all the windows in this place."

If I Knew Of A Land
© W.L. Hopper
Public Domain

His Eye Is On The Sparrow
© Charles H Gabriel, Civilla D Martin
Public Domain

Kneel At The Cross
© Charles E Moody
Public Domain

When He Reached Down His Hand For Me
© G. E. Wright
Public Domain

What A Friend We Have In Jesus
© Joseph Scriven, Charles Converse
Public Domain

Eyes Of Love
© Rhonda Hanson
Grace Under Pressure Publishing

Surrender
© Rhonda Hanson
Grace Under Pressure Publishing

Friend Of God
© Rhonda Hanson
Grace Under Pressure Publishing

I Will Walk With You
© Rhonda Hanson
Grace Under Pressure Publishing